D0235426

By the same author

The Defence Diaries of W. Morgan Petty

EUROPEAN ENTRIES

ENTRIES

THE COMMON
MARKET
PAPERS OF

W. Morgan Petty

EDITED BY BRIAN BETHELL

VIKING

VIKING

Penguin Books Ltd, Harmondsworth, Middlesex, England
Viking Penguin Inc., 40 West 23rd Street, New York, New York 10010, U.S.A.
Penguin Books Australia Ltd, Ringwood, Victoria, Australia
Penguin Books Canada Ltd, 2801 John Street, Markham, Ontario, Canada L3R 1B4
Penguin Books (N.Z.) Ltd, 182–190 Wairau Road, Auckland 10, New Zealand

First published 1985

Filmset in 11/13 Monophoto Baskerville by
Northumberland Press Ltd, Gateshead,
Tyne and Wear

Printed in Great Britain by
Richard Clay (The Chaucer Press) Ltd
Bungay, Suffolk

British Library Cataloguing in Publication Data
Bethell, Brian
  European entries: the Common Market papers of
  W. Morgan Petty
  I. Title
  823'.914[F]   PR6052.E/

  ISBN 0–670–80360–x

L'Angleterre est une nation de boutiquiers . . .
Du sublime au ridicule il n'y a qu'un pas . . .

Napoleon Bonaparte

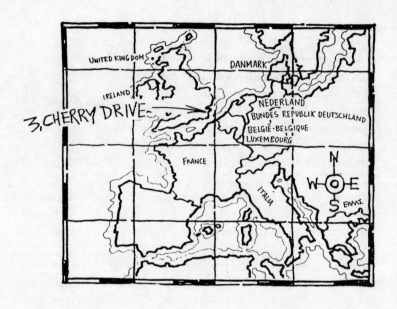

Friday, 2 March 1984

Roger and I set about rebuilding the garden shed. The cause of the explosion and subsequent fire which destroyed it still remain unclear. I think that we are both secretly convinced that a spark from Mr Bridger's celebratory bonfire was at the root of the trouble although he strenuously denies this and is adamant that sabotage is to blame. After lunch I hold a briefing session on our progress, or more truthfully our lack of progress, in joining NATO. I am surprised that we have still not received even a membership form. Roger suggests that our chances of joining might be improved by cementing a firmer relationship between ourselves and Europe and that we might achieve this by becoming members of the Common Market. I must admit that I am not quite sure where this market is held or what gets sold there. Most likely, as its name implies, it is held on a common, but which one? There must be dozens of them scattered about Europe and we couldn't just load the Morris Minor up and set out in the hope of running across it. I shall have to give the matter some thought.

Saturday, 3 March

We normally get our eggs from Norman, a friend of Letitia Odette. He keeps a dozen or so Rhode Island Reds and is more than happy to sell the surplus. Unfortunately, due to a nearby outbreak of something called Newcastle's disease, he has had to wring their necks, and we have been forced back to purchasing them from the supermarket. Roger and Letitia Odette, whom he had given a lift to the shops, return somewhat dismayed. Surprise number one was to discover that since their last visit to the egg stand the terms Small, Medium and Large have disappeared under the influence of this Common Market to be replaced by sizes one to seven. Surprise number two was to see these new sizes displayed in boxes of fifteen, something which when Roger inquired the girl at the till referred to as a 'Euro dozen'. I am not sure that it was wise for Roger to ask, if that was the case, could he have a Euro half-dozen, as the young lady, clearly displeased, slammed the box of eggs on to the sunflower oil with such force that both items broke.

Sunday, 4 March

Over a breakfast of bacon and extremely small eggs (Roger bought number sevens but we have since learned that Euro-eggs, unlike almost everything else – hat and shoe sizes, etc. – actually get smaller the higher the number) we decide that 3 Cherry Drive, Canterbury, should participate in this Common Market. Who knows, if enough people turn up when we're there we might even make some money for our Defence Fund. The biggest problem now is how to go about it. Do we join as individual members or *en bloc*? Roger suggests a note to Roy Jenkins, who I remember as that very jolly, red-faced man who used to be in charge of the police force but Roger says has more recently been employed giving away money to French farmers. I am further surprised to learn that he was also a founder member of the S.D.P. I had always rather suspected that Dr David Owen and Mr Oliver, our old friend who went off to open a tea-shop in Norfolk, were the only two paid-up members. Now we know of at least three. I expect Mr Jenkins will enjoy his rest in the House of Commons after Europe, for Roger says if running the Common Market is anything like as difficult as his uncle Rupert's organizing of boot fairs for the Barn Owl Preservation Society he will have been up very early in all weathers telling everybody where to put their stalls and sorting out disputes over parking. It may be some time since he hung up his peaked cap and clipboard, but he should still be able to fill us in on the basic details, such as the availability of vacant pitches and, most important, where the next of these Common Markets is to be held.

Tuesday, 6 March

I spend the afternoon drawing up a list of possible things to sell on our stall should we be fortunate enough to get one. Roger, having recently read several books on the subject, says he is keen to become a 'purveyor of objets d'art' – scent bottles, framed prints, etc. However, much to his annoyance, I insist that we concentrate, at least at first, on areas in which we have some practical experience and propose that we should instead sell vegetables, especially cos lettuce, which we produce in great abundance. We could extend this, should there prove to be the demand, to include home-made jams and pasties which the Odette sisters who live nearby would be happy to make. I was explaining our plan to Mr Bridger, who prunes most of the trees locally, when he called in with a load of apple logs. He responded quite bluntly that we should have nothing to do with them on the other side, by which I suppose he means Europe. At first I put this down to his well-known dislike of all things foreign begun by Mrs Bridger running off with an Italian carpet salesman and setting up home in Bolton and reinforced by the French-inspired ban on the growing of King Edward potatoes. However, while he was stacking the wood he reeled off a very long list of disturbing facts concerning the imposition of European agricultural quotas. He did not know if there was such a quota for cos lettuce, which is unfortunate, as one packet of seed can, under Roger's expert care, produce several hundred sturdy young plants. I shall have to make inquiries.

Saturday, 10 March

Roger has certainly embraced our new European adventure with gusto. This morning when he arrived to prick out the cauliflowers he was wearing a striped jersey and a beret. Unfortunately the beret, which he says was left over from his Scouting days, is far too big and keeps slipping down over his eyes. Surely his head could not have shrunk in the intervening period? The most likely explanation is that the material has stretched with age. Another problem was that he had dyed it black and the colour was not fast. Thus when he removed it from his head to wipe the sweat from his face he took on a startling resemblance to Mr Al Jolson in the film *The Jazz Singer*. I have written to Sir Richard Butler, the President of the National Farmers' Union, on the vexed question of vegetable sizes, for it appears that, as well as being restricted in what you may grow, the end product must also be of the right dimensions. Thus for example if your dwarf runner beans should be an eighth of an inch too long, or your carrots a millimetre beyond the permitted diameter, you cannot sell them. I know that horticultural technology has improved considerably in recent years, but growing things to these tolerances does seem a little excessive even for a gardening craftsman like Roger. I have also asked Sir Richard for guidance on lettuce, tomatoes and celery, as we wouldn't want to make the long journey to this market only to be turned away.

Wednesday, 14 March

Ingrid, Roger's friend the feminist poet, arrives very agitated. She is, she says, somewhat dismayed to learn that we are planning to join the Common Market without full consideration of the feminist angle. Quite what this is neither Roger nor myself are sure. But to stop things getting heated I tell Ingrid that if she cares to explain we will listen, even though we have some urgent things to do in the garden. The silence was I think quite instructive. In order to placate Roger over the 'objet d'art' business I have agreed to set aside a small area on our stall for the sale of plaster busts of famous people. His plan is to produce these himself in the garden shed, and to that end he has already acquired two moulds, those of Winston Churchill and Bobby Robson. The only drawback is that we have still not completed the repairs to the shed, especially the roof – something I have been putting off because of the high cost of felt. We were just discussing what could be done about this when Letitia Odette arrived with some very nice-looking home-made liver pâté. Letitia – who takes the *Financial Times* to keep abreast of the progress of her shares in Marks and Spencers, and is for that reason something of a fiscal expert – explains that our impending membership of the Common Market should help solve this problem, as they are well known for spending grant money faster than a drunken sailor. If this is the case I shall also approach them for help with a new greenhouse, for our present one is very old and the heater so unreliable that last year a fault in the thermostat led to Roger's melons wilting badly. I have addressed this second inquiry to a Mr David Curry, who is Chairman of something called the Common Market's agricultural standing committee, though I must confess why this committee should stand puzzles me. Perhaps Letitia Odette is right and there are so many officials connected with this Common Market that they have simply run out of chairs.

Tuesday, 20 March

The more I delve into the workings of this Common Market the more I find to commend it. Why only this morning I discovered that along with membership go exclusive fishing rights to something called 'European waters'. I must confess that at first I was a little sceptical but, as Roger points out, many Scottish crofters enjoy ancient rights to salmon rivers in the Highlands, and this is probably something similar. I have therefore asked whether there are any prior claims on the two hundred yards, or if they insist on Continental measurements – two hundred metres – west of the Admiralty Pier, Dover. Roger tells me that, in his younger days, he fished this stretch of water regularly with rod and line, with some success. I am also anxious to know whether these rights include shellfish, which I suspect the area might provide in abundance, and there are few things I enjoy more than a freshly boiled whelk.

Saturday, 31 March

The first post brings a note from the Right Honourable Roy Jenkins. It seems that he enjoyed my letter very much but had no idea how to reply to it. A few hints on hygiene and trading regulations would certainly have done for a start. I spend the afternoon looking through the pages of *The Pictorial History of the World with Dates*, a relic of my schooldays, which I hope will throw some light on possible market sites. Unfortunately the pages concerned with Europe have, with time, turned quite a nasty brown colour – a process accelerated no doubt by an accident with a mug of cocoa while I was studying for matriculation – which now makes definition difficult. I have just pencilled in what I hope is an accurate position for Utrecht (Treaty signed 1713, Philip V acknowledged King of Spain) and am plotting the whereabouts of Nantes (Edict 1598 grants Protestants liberty of private worship) when I am startled by the sound of a loud car horn in the street outside playing 'Colonel Bogey'. I have only ever known one person to possess such an instrument, and my worst fears are confirmed when I open the door to discover Mr Oliver. It appears that the tea-shop business has come to a sticky end and he is back in Canterbury seeking work. From what I can make out Master Hardiman, his 'partner' in the venture, has gone off to teach yoga in one of Her Majesty's Prisons. Mr Oliver asks if Roger is in, but fortunately he has taken the mower to have the rotor blades sharpened. Unfortunately, Mr Oliver says he will call back. I must confess I don't like the sound of this at all.

THE RT HON ROY JENKINS MP

HOUSE OF COMMONS
LONDON SWIA OAA

30th March, 1984

Dear Mr Petty,

    I enjoyed your letter very much,
but I am afraid I have no idea how to
reply to it!

                  Yours sincerely,

                    Roy Jenkins

W. Morgan Petty Esq.
3 Cherry Drive
Canterbury
Kent

Thursday, 5 April

A quick inspection of the seed propagator causes me great concern. Roger, his enthusiasm carrying him away, has planted five trays of cos lettuce – nearly a thousand seedlings! Heaven knows where we will plant them and what we will do with them afterwards. The sharpness of my rebuke causes him to go into one of his moods, and he is still sulking when Ingrid arrives with her friend Jaz. Jaz, it seems, is the publicity officer for Ingrid's women's group WAVE (Women Against Virtually Everything), and her function, so Ingrid says, is to 'tell women what it's really like to be a woman'. Unfortunately it appears that Jaz, as well as being the publicity officer, is also dyslexic – something that became apparent to the other members when she set about painting the slogan DOWN WITH MEN on a wall only for it to end up reading WONW TIDE HMEN. However, this does not seem to have damped her enthusiasm for the task, and she is currently translating one of Ingrid's poems, 'Northumberland Superwoman', into Italian.

The purpose of their visit concerned the sale of Roger's plaster ornaments. Ingrid and Jaz feel that, in the interests of sexual equality, alongside Messrs Robson and Churchill there should also be plaster ornaments of female figures. My suggestion that Marilyn Monroe might sell well was met with a look of pure horror. Ingrid insists that moulds be found depicting suffragettes chaining themselves to railings or throwing themselves under Derby runners, but where? By chance I learn from Roger that a Luisa Cinciari-Rodano chairs something called the Committee of Inquiry into the Situation of Women in Europe. I drop her a line immediately in the hope that she may know where such moulds can be obtained and thus help me out of a very difficult situation. I note that this particular Common Market committee does not stand. How polite of them to have given chairs to the ladies.

Mr Oliver has got a job in public relations. I am not quite sure of all the details, but it seems to involve taking rather large parties of camera-wielding Japanese tourists around the cathedral. It also involves his wearing a mauve uniform jacket, which did not blend well with the ghastly green shirt he had on when he called in at lunchtime. Roger had just finished his first attempt at plaster modelling, and although Mr Churchill looked all right, the mould of Bobby Robson had, for some reason, tilted over to one side, and as a consequence the manager of the England soccer team had a completely flat head, and an arm missing. Mr Oliver's jocular remark that a great many people probably didn't know what Mr Robson looked like anyway and so wouldn't notice was not well received, and Roger, flushed, turned down his subsequent invitation to join him on the Camera Club's summer outing to Skegness. I know for a fact that Roger was very much looking forward to this, and in a fit of pique has cut off his nose to spite his face.

Sunday, 8 April

I spend a very pleasant day, in the company of Letitia Odette, at an exhibition of paintings. On view are two of Roger's water-colours, 'Thrush at First Light' and 'Autumn – Herne Bay Pier'. Much to my surprise Letitia purchases 'Contemplating Infinity'. I tell her that ten pounds seems an awful lot to pay for a sheet of hardboard covered in irregular black and white triangles and ask her whether she sees it as an investment? However it turns out that 'Contemplating Infinity' is just the right size to cover a damp patch on the chimneybreast in her dining room. Over a cup of tea and potted meat paste sandwiches Letitia suggests that we might draw closer to the countries of Europe if we were to involve ourselves more fully in their cultural life. I must say that I think this is a splendid idea, and, given the inspiration of the

15

afternoon's surroundings, can think of no better way to do this than to hold our own European art exhibition at 3 Cherry Drive, the pictures on show being those produced from the artists of member countries, past and present.

Once home I draw up a list of the museums and art galleries most likely to contain the cream of this work – the Louvre in Paris, the Rijksmuseum in Amsterdam, etc. – and write straight away requesting to borrow some pictures. On Roger's advice I ask the former for 'Post-Impressionist' works by Toulouse-Lautrec, who he says was a French dwarf with a passion for painting women of dubious character, and the latter for canvases by Rembrandt, a Dutchman with a fondness for depicting fat ladies with nothing on. I have assured the Directors of these august institutions that we will take very good care of any pictures they do lend us and that, if their generosity leaves them with blank spaces on their wall, I am sure that Roger would be only too happy to loan them, in return, some of his water-colours for the duration.

Monday, 9 April

The post brings two letters and a handbill. The first missive is from Christopher Jackson M.E.P. I wrote to him with a number of questions, including details on how best Roger should go about presenting his Champion Bedfordshires (onions which are the envy of the Gardening Club) for the European Market. While his letter seems in the main to be optimistic, I am confused by some of the detail. I shall have to study it more closely. The second letter is from the Embassy of the Polish People's Republic. I wrote to them concerning our possible surplus of cos lettuce, asking if they were interested in purchasing some of the over-production. The idea was Letitia Odette's; she said that it was the done thing to sell off surpluses produced by Common Market members to Eastern European countries. Unfortunately the Polish reply is in the negative as it seems that Poland, like us here at 3 Cherry Drive, is strapped for cash. I shall therefore try Czechoslovakia in the hope that (a) they are fond of cos lettuce and (b) they have a little more in the bank. The handbill is from Ingrid inviting us to VSIDTY OT SIS ERSTHE TIGANGOL. Jaz's work, I think, though heaven knows what it means. I just hope it isn't urgent.

Tuesday, 10 April

At first light, armed with his fishing-rod, some freshly dug lugworms, courtesy of Mr Bridger's brother Arthur (himself a keen fisherman), and a thermos flask of hot coffee Roger set off for Dover. A day of which he had high hopes was soured early on by a brush with the pier-keeper. Apparently this gentleman insisted that Roger pay a fee for fishing there, and despite his protestations that these were Common Market waters and thus freely open to us, he had eventually to pay his forty pence. This episode was later compounded by the fact that he did not catch a single fish and, having left his oilskins at home by mistake, got very wet when it rained all afternoon. I had already made the fresh breadcrumbs and batter when he returned, but seeing no sign of a sagging bag of fish, only his own somewhat dishevelled appearance and downcast look as he came up the garden path, I thought it prudent to put these away for later use.

Wednesday, 11 April

It is indeed, as the proverb says, an ill wind that blows no good. By first post I receive a letter from the Private Secretary of Mr Enoch Powell. This was in reply to a note I sent him late last month about wet fish. At that time, having just learned of the Common Market fisheries policy and confident that, let loose on his own stretch of the English Channel, Roger would more than fill the freezer, I considered adding fish to our list of items for sale. However such a policy would certainly have required another pair of hands. Mr Bridger mentioned that Mr Powell was very much against member-

Member
of the European Parliament

W Morgan Petty Esq   30th March 1984
3 Cherry Drive
Canterbury
Kent

Dear Mr Petty

Thank you for your letter of 7th March. It is good to see that the
independence of spirit which made Britain great coupled with, if I may say
so, a streak of sturdy mercantilism are surviving in Kent. Hengist (or
was it Horsa?) would be proud of you.

You raise some important points about weapons procurement and saving costs
and I am asking the Secretary of State for Defence (though I know he will
respect your independence) for his views on this, particularly the novel
possibility at which you only hinted for the use of 1914-18 bayonets against
nuclear weapons. I have also asked Lord Carrington in his new capacity as
Secretary-General of NATO how you should go about joining.

Regarding the Common Market, there seemed recently some risk of it being
postponed. Unfortunately there was trouble with disruptive elements last
time (if only we had had some of Mrs Oddete's pasties it might have preserved
better humour). Apart from problems with requests for changes in the bye-laws
(particularly regarding fees for participation) there are difficulties over
quantities being sold and a severe shortage of milk churns. However, the
onions sound a good idea and would be handy if it comes to a fight.

However, when it is working, the Market is the best there is and offers big
sales opportunities so you may, despite the problems, like to put your name
forward for a stall. Stalls are not fixed in number but existing stallholders
are very particular about newcomers and it usually takes some years to come in
(watch the fees in advance!). While I am sure Roger's Champion Bedfordshires
are excellent, I have to confess the French are very sensitive about competition
and it might be wise not to advertise your prowess in advance. Regarding
size, which could well be used as a non-tariff barrier, may I suggest you
grow large onions which you can peel down to the desired size using slip-on
skins which I am sure some neighbour would be pleased to manufacture?

I wish you good fortune in your endeavours.

Yours sincerely

Christopher M Jackson MEP

AMBASADA
POLSKIEJ RZECZYPOSPOLITEJ LUDOWEJ
BIURO RADCY HANDLOWEGO
w Londynie
EMBASSY OF THE POLISH PEOPLE'S REPUBLIC
COMMERCIAL COUNSELLOR'S OFFICE
in London

Telegraphic Address: Morhan G
Telephone: 01-580 5481-6

15, Devonshire Street
LONDON W1N 2AR

Nasz znak   Wasz znak
Our ref.   Your ref.   ..4th..of..April..............198....4

W.Morgan Petty Esg.
3, Cherry Drive,
Canterbury, Kent.

Dear Sir,

We acknowledge with thanks the receipt of your very kind letter
dated March 16th.
Unfortunatelby as you may aware, our country is currently under
preasure of lack of foreign currencies for importation.
That's why, we cannot forsee in the near future any promising
possibilities for exporters of food to Poland.
Should the situation change we shell be more then happy to get in
touch with your goodselves.

Yours faithfully

M.Rózga
D-ty Commercial Attache

ship of this Common Market, and Viola Odette speculated that he might have bought something there with which he was dissatisfied and the seller wouldn't change it. I know that she had a very similar experience in a dress-shop some thirty years ago and never went near the place again. It therefore occurred to me that we might kill two birds with one stone and offer the Northern Ireland M.P. the chance to help us and at the same time see things from the seller's point of view. Perhaps it might even change his mind. I must confess that I do not know how knowledgeable Mr Powell is on the subject of wet fish, but I told him not to worry as Roger only expected to catch cod and whiting, which are easily distinguishable. I did however mention that it would be a big help if he could bring his own apron. Fortunately his secretary is not specific as to whether Mr Powell would like to come, which is a relief, for if he had agreed and Roger's subsequent performances with rod and line were as dismal as yesterday's there would be nothing for him to sell.

Friday, 13 April

Roger has developed shivers and a sore throat. I was searching through the shed for the ingredients for a paraffin chest-poultice when to my horror I discovered two more trays of cos lettuce hidden under a table. We have more than enough already, and no word of reply yet from the Czechoslovakian government. From the size of the plants I suspect them to have been planted at the same time as the other five and hidden so as to minimize the offence. I confront the ailing Roger with the evidence, whereupon his sore throat rapidly becomes laryngitis, and when I continue to press for an explanation he, red-faced, croaks out something about a failure of communication. If it is communication that he wants, then communication he shall have, if only to stop the place being taken over by lettuce. I have erected a large noticeboard with the words 'European Matters Only' which I shall instruct Roger to read each morning before starting

From: The Rt·Hon. J. Enoch Powell, MBE, MP

HOUSE OF COMMONS
LONDON SWIA OAA

10th April 1984

Dear Mr Petty,

    Mr Powell has asked me to thank you for
your letter of 25th March, posted 5th April,
and to say that he appreciated the points
which you made.

Yours sincerely,

Monica Wilson (Mrs)

Private Secretary

W. Morgan Petty, Esq.,
3 Cherry Drive,
Canterbury,
Kent.

work. On this I have placed CHERRY DRIVE EURODIREC-
TIVE NUMBER ONE. The message is simple: 'No cos lettuce
until further notice.' Laryngitis or no laryngitis, this should
forestall any further failure of communication. Despite his
being poorly I am passing the french windows when I notice
Roger down at the end of the garden. He is hurriedly emptying
seed trays and digging in the contents. Message received loud
and clear, I think.

Saturday, 14 April

Rain. No work in the garden today. The post brings a letter
from Sir Richard Butler, President of the National Farmers'
Union. Apparently we, along with the rest of Kent, have
already been fully integrated into membership of this Common Market. I am surprised that no one saw fit to write and
tell us, and even more so that we have not been sent a
membership card. Roger suggests that it may have been
pushed through the door while we were out and got mixed up
with the dozens of double-glazing brochures and *Reader's
Digest* book offers. I do hope not. I remember the fuss there
was getting a replacement for his library tickets which he left
in the pocket of his corduroy trousers – something we only
discovered after two washes and a rinse at temperature setting
six.

The afternoon brings a visit from Viola Odette. We have
not seen a great deal of her lately as her legs have been playing
her up. Her sister Letitia has told her all about our plans for
an art exhibition and she is very excited by the prospect.
However she explains that if we are serious about involving
ourselves in European culture then it would be a mistake to
ignore one of its major annual milestones, and to that end she
suggests that we enter the Eurovision Song Contest. I cannot
honestly say I have heard of this, but according to Viola it is
a singing competition between groups of blonde-haired young
people in tight trousers and short skirts. Despite my voicing
misgivings about the logistics and expense of undertaking two

AGRICULTURE HOUSE · KNIGHTSBRIDGE · LONDON SW1X 7NJ

01-235 5077

THE
NATIONAL FARMERS'
UNION

FROM THE PRESIDENT

SIR RICHARD BUTLER

10th April, 1984

W. Morgan Petty Esq.,
3 Cherry Drive,
Canterbury,
Kent.

Dear Mr Petty,

Thank you for your letter which my secretary has already
acknowledged on my behalf.

You certainly seem to be a most resourceful individual
with organising ability to effectively protect your own
interests. As President of the NFU I am of course pleased
to receive direct confirmation that some of this country's
urban dwellers share the independence of spirit so
characteristic of many farmers and growers in this country.
Abilities which have been harnessed in finding solutions to
the numerous challenges which UK membership of the
European Economic Community has raised. Alone these
challenges are difficult, but it is the role of the NFU to
protect the interests of its membership against such
challenges through effective representations to both Her
Majesty's Government and the European Economic Community.
Regular briefing of MPs and Members of the European
Parliament is essential.

It is against this background that your proposal to join
the ten-member European Economic Community should be
considered. Community regulations affect the production,
marketing and distribution of all fruit and vegetables and
provide a measure of Community protection against imports
from non-Member countries. Kent is a fully integrated part
of the United Kingdom and is therefore already within
membership. Your suggestion to apply for membership,
therefore, has been overtaken by events.

Yours sincerely,

Richard Butler

such prestigious ventures at the same time, Viola insists (I cannot but feel an element of oneupmanship is present here – though close, the sisters have always been very competitive), and in the end I write a short note to Mr Bill Cotton, the Managing Director of B.B.C. Television, asking for any guidance that he is able to give. In order to save money I have suggested that they might like to hold the song contest here, and Viola confirms that she would be happy to lay on a light buffet for the other performers. This is very generous but (as Roger explains later) not totally altruistic, as it might provide a chance for her to meet Terry Wogan – a name new to me, but whose radio programme Viola listens to while the home chiropodist does her feet.

Monday, 16 April

Roger is adamant that, as our proposed representative in the song contest, he is prepared to wear the tight trousers, but is equally adamant that he will not dye his hair. Pleas to his sense of *communitaire* spirit went, I am afraid, unheeded. As Viola thinks it so vital that we do participate in this contest I decided on a less direct and more subtle approach. For our mid-morning coffee break I opened a packet of Garibaldi biscuits, Roger's favourites, and gilded the lily with an alternative of chocolate fingers. I had just settled back in my chair, and was running over all the arguments in favour of hair-dyeing, when I heard the shed door slam and the loud use of a word I would most certainly not care to repeat in print. The reason for this outburst was that Roger's second batch of plaster ornaments has fared no better than the first. This time it is the model of Winston Churchill that has suffered, the wartime Prime Minister taking on a remarkable resemblance to Charles Laughton in *The Hunchback of Notre Dame*. I thought of suggesting to Roger that he re-label it as such, but I cannot recall at any point in that particular film the hunchback smoking a cigar.

Friday, 20 April

A letter from the B.B.C. It seems that we are too late to enter this year's Eurovision Song Contest, and a further complication is that the song must be an original work. This is a great nuisance as I had high hopes of Roger's rendering of 'A Wandering Minstrel I' and am not sure how we will replace it. Roger spends the morning sorting out his seed runner beans, of which he seems to have rather a lot. Not being sure of their popularity on the Continent and anxious to avoid a repeat of the lettuce fiasco, I think it would be a good idea to issue Cherry Drive Eurodirective Number Two on this subject.

Mr Oliver arrives with a foreign gentleman, Monsieur Charles Bettiger. It appears that in the absence of Japanese tourists Mr Oliver has spent the week escorting a party of Belgians. Monsieur Bettiger, or Charlie as he says we should call him, works for the Common Market in Brussels, and Mr Oliver, knowing of our interest (and I suspect anxious to get back into Roger's good books), brought him to meet us. Our very first contact with the Eurocrats, as Roger calls them. In celebration, although early, we open a bottle of oak-leaf wine. After a few glasses I discover, much to my disappointment, that Charlie, far from being a high-powered Common Market executive, is in fact a lift maintenance man at one of the administrative offices and has little more knowledge of the set-up there than we ourselves. However on one subject, the Common Market position on whaling and the importation of whale products, his knowledge is encyclopedic – a legacy of having once spent five hours freeing a Soviet delegation to the Market who had become trapped between floors. On his departure Charlie and myself exchange addresses and I promise that we will look him up just as soon as our European business takes us to Brussels.

TELEPHONE 01-743 8000   TELEX: 265781   TELEGRAMS AND CABLES: TELECASTS LONDON TELEX

13 April 1984

Dear Mr Morgan Petty

Your letter addressed to Mr Cotton has been passed to
our office.

If a person wants to submit a song for the Eurovision
Song Contest, they must send their material in the
first instance to the Music Publishers Association.
If their material is lucky enough to be selected, they
then take part in the Song for Europe contest, from
which one entry is chosen to go forward and
represent Britain in the Eurovision Song Contest.
It is too late for you to take part in the 1984
contest, but if you wish to do so for next year,
all entries should be with the Music Publishers
Association by September or October of this year.

May I suggest, therefore, that you write or telephone
the Music Publishers Association to find out more
details. Their address and telephone number is as
follows:

Music Publishers Association
7th Floor
Kingsway House
103 Kingsway
London
WC2B 6QX

With best wishes -

Yours sincerely

John Howard Davies
Head of Light Entertainment Group, Television

Mr W Morgan Petty
3 Cherry Drive
Canterbury
Kent

Thursday, 26 April

For five days now Roger and Viola Odette have been closeted
in the living room preparing our Song for Europe. Despite
my heavy hints that there are more immediate things to be
done in the garden, the morning is full of snatches of the piano
and the practising of scales. At lunchtime they enter the
kitchen, their faces alight with smiles of triumph, to inform
me that they have written a certain winner, 'The Goldfish
Song'. I must admit to having been somewhat taken aback
by what I consider to be a ridiculous title, but Viola, who has
made a close study of the contest, tells me that it was actually
won one year by something called 'Boom Bang a Bang'. If
that is the case, then 'The Goldfish Song' doesn't sound so
odd after all. I listen to a spirited rendition and must confess
I am left speechless, something which unfortunately both
Roger and Viola take as a sign of approval. I am also distressed
to learn that they have 'come up with a little gimmick',
something which Viola thinks is an essential element in this
contest. The idea is to dress Roger in the gold lamé jacket
which her son Reginald's late wife bought him in 1959 after
insisting he enter a Liberace look-alike contest, thus carrying
the theme of gold over from song to appearance.

Monday, 30 April

A letter from Mrs Barbara Castle. I approached her some
time ago on the subject of our cos lettuces. Her reply is that
the likelihood of purchase by the Common Market of the
surplus is remote, and she suggests instead a switch to lupin
production, as these, it seems, are soon to benefit financially
as part of an official Common Market scheme. I receive this
news as a mixed blessing. Roger is certainly something of an
expert on lupin cultivation – his Miss Micklethwaite and Pixie
Delights are annual prizewinners – but with still no answer
from behind the Iron Curtain, we are left with the problem
of what to do with all the lettuce.

Rehearsals of 'The Goldfish Song' continue. Passing the living room I hear what I think is called an 'up-tempo' version. While I know that Roger will not actually be performing this until 1985, my own candid and perhaps unkind view is that, given its present rate of progress, any public performance before the end of the decade could prove embarrassing.

Wednesday, 2 May

An extremely busy day. Roger is in the garden and, in between a little light weeding, has started the construction of the stands for our Euro art exhibition. I for my part am continuing the equally demanding administration of the project. Certainly there is a lot to be done – the printing of posters and tickets, organizing extra cups and saucers and, more importantly with some of the more modern and what Roger calls non-representational art, making sure the pictures are actually hanging up the right way. It is on the third point that I become a bit stuck. I have always thought, perhaps naively, that the up side of a painting was obvious. However a glance through Roger's copy of *Modern Art – Blowing Your Mind With Paint* convinced me I was wrong. What looks like a fried egg on a plate of green cornflakes turns out to be in fact a portrait of the artist's mother, and I would most certainly not like to cause offence by hanging this or any other poor lady upside down. I have therefore turned for guidance to someone who, I am quite sure, would never make such a silly mistake: Sir Hugh Casson, President of the Royal Academy of Arts. Outlining my plans for the exhibition, I have asked Sir Hugh whether he could pop down and give us a few hints and maybe, if he has a few hours to spare, help Roger knock in some nails.

The afternoon post brings a very disappointing reply from the Rijksmuseum in Amsterdam. It appears that they cannot help, the best example of a Rembrandt painting of a fat lady with nothing on being in the Ermitage Museum, Leningrad. I have therefore dropped them a note requesting its loan.

Member
of the European Parliament

From Rt Hon Barbara Castle MEP
2 Queen Anne's Gate
London SW1

28 April 84

Mr W Morgan Petty
3 Cherry Drive
Canterbury
Kent

Dear Mr Morgan Petty

Thank you very much for your interesting letter of 6th March.
Please accept my apologies for the very long delay in replying
to you. This is because I have been absolutely inundated with
letters and meetings of late and consequently my correspondence
has fallen into arrears because of frequent absences tending my
tall at The Common Market, which is held in a number of different
European towns and entails much transportation of goods.

I am, of course, immensely pleased to learn that you have declared
your garden a nuclear free ~one since the proliferation of such
zones is of the utmost importance for the survival of our British
vegetables. I am pleased to be able to say that, after serious
and prolonged consultation with my dogs, my own garden, including
the raspberries, is now also proudly flourishing safely under the
nuclear free label.

As far as The Common Market is concerned, I am sorry to have to
say that the likelihood of automatic and unconditional purchase
of the end-product of your two packets of lettuce seeds is rather
remote, and you may therefore, as the fine summer progresses, indeed
find yourself the proprietor of a lettuce foothill this year, albeit
a non-nuclear one. However if you were to consider a switch to
lupins, I have it on the highest authority from Brussels that you
should benefit financially as part of the official Common Market
scheme for lupin seeds. There are rumours, too, of aid for
hyacinths, which some say have been re-classified as a vegetable,
but of this I have no firm news.

Should you be taking your lupins to market later in the year you may
find a ready exchange for olives, peaches, tomatoes and other
products produced to excess in Greece, which also has a nuclear-free
garden.

I do hope this clarifies the official position for you.

Yours sincerely

Barbara Castle

They can after all only say no. I forget to mention this small setback to Roger as I do not want to dampen his enthusiasm for making the picture stands.

Thursday, 3 May

Another disaster for Roger and his modelling project. I sensed success when he first removed the figures from the moulds, as they looked perfect in every detail. However some six hours later they were still wet, and a quick examination of the instructions on the box containing the model-making mixture confirmed an error in its preparation. Roger's attempt to overcome this by drying them beside an electric fire was without doubt a mistake. Still, we have managed to vacuum up most of the fragments now, and the dark stain that the explosion left on the kitchen wall has almost gone. The experience has however left him in a deep sulk; I think he rather thought this, his third attempt, would be lucky. To cheer him up, and also to prevent a repetition of the day's combustible events, I suggest that he might attempt his next models using papier mâché.

It is while we are cutting up the strips of old newspapers that my eye alights on an article in a several-weeks-old copy of the *Guardian* concerning the Elgin Marbles. These, it appears, were brought back many years ago by a Lord Elgin from a holiday in Greece and later given to the British Museum. Now the present Greek government are asking for their return, and the whole thing has turned into a rather nasty row. I tell Roger that this all seems a great deal of fuss over a few pieces of glass, and surely it could be resolved by the intervention of good sense. I know that Letitia has a paperweight of a Spanish flamenco dancer which turns into a snowstorm if you shake it, that her nephew brought her back from a package tour to Benidorm. I suppose this would be very much the modern-day equivalent of these Elgin Marbles, and although I know she has grown very attached to it, if the Spanish government (soon to be, like ourselves,

R IJ K S M U S E U M

HD 84.3593   **AMSTERDAM,** April 27, 1984
MS

Mr. W. Morgan Petty
3, Cherry Drive
Canterbury, Kent
ENGLAND

Dear Mr. Petty,

Thank you for your letter of April 11, 1984.

The ideas you unfold in your letter are most interesting,
especially where the home made jams and pasties are concerned.
I think that is exactly what the Common Market needs.
I would prefer strawberry jam myself, produced from the
fruits of Strawberry Fields, a well-known place in Liverpool
if I remember well.

As far as your request for the loan of a Rembrandt painting
is concerned, I am sorry to inform you that the Rijksmuseum
collection does not include any fat lady with nothing on;
the best specimen of this type is to be found in the Ermitage
in Leningrad (U.S.S.R.), but I doubt if the Sovjet-Union
would be prepared to enter the Common Market just for the
purpose of your exhibition.

                                    Yours sincerely,

                                    Dr. S.H. Levie
                                    Director General

members of the Common Market) asked for this back, I am sure that, in the interests of international harmony, she would gladly give it. Roger's explanation, with which I sadly have to agree, is that when people take up entrenched positions good sense is very often, like truth in wartime, the first casualty.

We have just begun soaking the newspaper in water when I am struck by the thought that there could be no better way for us to impress the other members of the Common Market than to solve this dispute between two member countries. Leaving Roger to continue the paper-tearing, I write straight away to Sir David Wilson at the British Museum and Melina Mercouri, the Greek Minister of Culture. I tell them that as a new member of the Common Market, and one with an impeccable reputation for impartiality, we would wish to help them in any way we could. After a great deal of serious thought, and following Solomon's example, I suggest that they compromise, dividing these Elgin Marbles up between them and, should there be an odd one left, tossing a coin for it. I suspect that in all the heat that this argument has engendered nobody will have given this, the obvious and practical solution, much thought. Incidentally I learn later that Ms Mercouri is an actress turned politician and am reminded of Roger's friend Clive. He too was in the theatre, being what is called in theatrical parlance a 'juvenile'. Clive was also very interested in politics, to the extent that he once stood, unsuccessfully, as a ratepayers' candidate in the local elections. The last Roger and myself heard of him he was a freelance interior designer in Morpeth. Who knows, if he had stuck with the politics he might have ended up Minister for the Arts.

Saturday, 5 May

The milk is late. Having used the last of yesterday's for a late-night, milky drink, I start the day with a cup of lemon tea. By coincidence the post brings a missive from the Emerald Isle on that very subject. In order to enjoy the many obvious advantages of Common Market membership members are, so I discover, obliged to trade principally with each other or incur penalties. With this in mind, and fond memories of the quality of Irish cream teas I enjoyed before the war, I wrote to Dr Fitzgerald, the Irish Prime Minister, or Taoiseach as they say over there, asking if, out of what I understand to be an extremely large milk surplus, and in the interests of European harmony, he could arrange for the delivery to us here at 3 Cherry Drive, Canterbury, of three pints of milk a day and a carton of double cream at weekends. Unfortunately the Taoiseach is unable to help because for some reason he thinks that Mrs Thatcher might object. I shall have to drop another note to Dr Fitzgerald making it quite clear that it is myself, and not Mrs Thatcher, who runs things at 3 Cherry Drive, and in any case I thought the idea behind this market was to encourage trade between members. I shall however, as the Taoiseach requests, send him a pot of Viola's very best home-made plum jam.

In the evening Roger and I settle down to watch the 1984 Eurovision Song Contest. Just as Viola had indicated, most of it consists of youngsters bobbing up and down to songs that sound remarkably similar. I was also struck by the number of these young people wearing shiny boots. My vote, if I had had one, would have gone to the man from Belgium who sounded as though his fingers were trapped in a door and he was being very brave about it. Roger offers an instant comparison at the end of the contest by singing an unaccompanied version of 'The Goldfish Song'. I do my best to smile, and retire to bed with a heavy heart, while Roger, now fully into the spirit and oblivious to my departure, continues with an encore.

Monday, 7 May

Ingrid arrives and tells me that she has brought us a present. I am first intrigued and then delighted to discover that it is a

| May, 1984.

Oifig an Taoisigh
Office of the Taoiseach

Mr. W. Morgan Petty,
3 Cherry Drive,
Canterbury,
Kent.

Dear Mr. Petty,

The Taoiseach, Dr. Garret FitzGerald, T.D., has asked me to reply to your recent letter and to say that it was as refreshing as a pint of (non-intervention) Irish dairy milk to read it.   Would that other citizens of the E.E.C. were as civic-minded as yourself, Roger and the Odette sisters.

As far as delivery of milk and cream to Cherry Drive is concerned, the Taoiseach would, ordinarily, have been delighted to accede to your request.   However, he does not think that your Prime Minister would welcome his intrusion into local British markets, and for that reason must regrettably disappoint you.   If, however, you wished to dispose of some surpluses of your own, he would love an occasional head of cabbage from Roger or a pot of jam from the Odette sisters. He hopes you will remember him to them.

Yours sincerely,

Private Secretary
to the Taoiseach.

Oifig an Taoisigh, Tithe an Rialtais, Baile Átha Cliath 2.
Office of the Taoiseach, Government Buildings, Dublin 2.

handcart. She tells us that its construction was undertaken by Spike, another of her friends from W A V E, who has just completed a Manpower Services course in joinery. She expresses the hope that having such a fine, new handcart will help us achieve maximum sales at the Common Market. I am sure it will, and how very kind of them both. The woodwork has been painted in such bright colours that I suspect even the costermongers I remember from my youth would envy us. Ingrid says that she was going to get Jaz to stencil 'W. Morgan Petty Vegetables by Appointment to the European Common Market' down one side, but it is our good fortune that the young lady is away for a fortnight's holiday 'defacing advertising posters that degrade women'. I pretend not to hear Roger, who does not get on at all well with Jaz, express the uncharitable hope that she will get caught.

Wednesday, 9 May

Despite my many letters to the Common Market I have, as yet, not received a word about a subsidy for the lupins grown here at 3 Cherry Drive. I do not think that someone as finely tuned to the deliberations of this institution as Mrs Castle could have made a mistake, and the hold-up is proving very irritating for Roger, who I know is anxious to begin planting. Having had no success with the Indians, so to speak, I decide that I shall deal directly with the chiefs, and to that end resolve to hold a meeting here at 3 Cherry Drive for the heads of government of Common Market countries. It will provide an opportunity for all of us to have what I think is called in political parlance 'full and frank discussions' and tie up any loose ends over our membership. By the evening I have composed letters to Wilfred Martens, Helmut Kohl, Rudolph Lubbers, etc. inviting them to get together here some time in the future. I am sure that, if I ask him, Mr Bridger will erect a barbecue, and I have no doubts at all that the Odette sisters would be happy to help out with the catering. There is however a problem over accommodation. Naturally the heads

35

of government will stay in the house, although a shortage of bedrooms will mean that they will have to share (all of course except Mrs Thatcher who, for obvious reasons, will have a room of her own), and I have therefore asked the various Prime Ministers to indicate in their replies whether they are smokers or non-smokers. Unfortunately we do not have enough accommodation inside for the hordes of security men which Letitia Odette, who popped in briefly, says hover around these get-togethers like flies. I shall therefore seek to hire a couple of bell-tents and have Roger erect these down by the gladioli. This will have the disadvantage of very limited access to the bathroom and mean that the occupants will have to ablute themselves with a hose run out from the garden standpipe. However I do not think this should cause too much of a problem, as I understand that these are the sort of men who think nothing of shaving with a blunt razor-blade and can kill with a single blow, and so I am confident that they will manage.

Saturday, 12 May

Today we have the first full-scale dress rehearsal of 'The Goldfish Song' (or 'La chanson du poisson d'or', as Viola calls it in her introduction), Roger, in extremely tight trousers, gold lamé jacket and wellington boots freshly aerosoled with silver paint, bobbing up and down almost in time with Viola's pounding on the cottage upright. After the performance, and the mending of Roger's trousers, which split after a particularly vigorous bob, the artistes celebrate with a glass of sherry while I slip away and browse through a copy of the *New Musical Express*, which I had bought in case of just such an emergency. Having glanced at several of the articles in search of the services of a professional song-writer, someone who is 'with it', as I believe the young people say, I discern that either Mr Elton John or Mr Paul McCartney would seem to be our best bet. I therefore drop each of these gentlemen a line, outlining my predicament and asking if they could, in

the parlance of the musical world, 'get something together'
for Roger to sing as our entry to next year's contest. I also ask
how much they would charge for such a service, explaining
that our funds, given the art exhibition as well, are somewhat
limited. I am sure that one of these young men will oblige and
may even be grateful for the opportunity to launch a new
composition on the music world in this way.

Monday, 14 May

By first post I receive a charming letter from the Music
Publishers' Association. The writer obviously shares my disquiet over 'The Goldfish Song' and then goes on to attempt,
for some reason, to dissuade us from Common Market participation altogether. It may well be that she knows something
that we do not. However, I am afraid that we are already too
deeply committed to pull out, having equipped the Morris
Minor with assorted phrase-books and converted the rear
passenger area into vegetable trays with little vinyl-covered
tables that slide out at the back to make serving counters.
Furthermore any such decision would jeopardize the possibility of grant aid from the various European funds.

Our first request for assistance was to the Committee
on Development and Co-operation. The earth that Roger
excavated for the defence command bunker down by the
rhododendrons still covers a large area of ground, and I have
therefore applied under one of the generous schemes open to
Common Market members for a sum of money to turn this
patch of so far derelict land into a recreational area for young
visitors. Viola Odette has taken to looking after her grandson
and granddaughter, Wayne and Cheryl, two afternoons a
week, and I know that they would find such a reclaimed area,
with a slide and a swing or two, most diverting while their
grandmother helps me out with the increasing amount of
paperwork that I have to deal with. Furthermore Roger says
that according to the *Guardian* there is also soon to be a big
share-out of Common Market funds, and the payments are

to be allocated on the basis of need. As we need everything from a new pair of wellingtons to an artificial ski slope (Roger has decided to take up skiing as part of his personal policy of European integration) I anticipate that we should get a very big slice of the financial cake. I calculate that we could spare as our contribution some fifteen pounds to this share-out, and hopefully would in return receive something akin to twenty thousand. I have therefore approached Dr David Owen to see if he will act as our representative in this matter, where I am sure the experience of wheeling and dealing that he gained as Foreign Secretary will be invaluable.

Tuesday, 15 May

A crisis. Letitia Odette who, as I have explained, reads the *Financial Times* to keep abreast of the progress of her shares in Marks and Spencers and is, for that reason, something of a fiscal expert, shows me a cutting she has taken from that newspaper. This explains that transactions at the Common Market are not carried out in ordinary money but in something called European currency units. What are we to do? For a start none of us knows what one of these European currency units looks like. Realizing the urgency of the matter, I did pop into the Midland Bank on the way back from buying Roger a new beret (I simply could not stand seeing his face streaked with dye any longer), but when I asked the girl behind the counter whether they had any European currency units she just stared blankly at me. Therefore on Letitia's advice I drop a line to Lord Barnett of Heywood and Royton, who she says before his elevation to the peerage was very big at the Treasury and who can still be seen from time to time on television broadcasting messages of gloom and doom about the economy. I have therefore asked Lord Barnett, as a man undoubtedly familiar with foreign currencies, if he could let us have a description of one of these currency units, and also the current rate of exchange to the pound sterling. I am sure his lordship will appreciate, just as we do, how irritating it is

THE MUSIC PUBLISHERS' ASSOCIATION LIMITED
103 KINGSWAY LONDON WC2B 6QX
TELEPHONE 01-831 7591/2/3

JAC/B5   11th May 1984

Mr. W. Morgan Petty
3 Cherry Drive
CANTERBURY
Kent

Dear Mr. Morgan Petty,

    Mr. White was at tea when your letter of 27th April arrived at this office
and having sensed some kind of urgency in your words, decided that an instant
reply was called for. I hope you will not feel slighted at a missive from a
mere assistant to the Association's General Secretary but I can assure you that
my aim is to please, and impart, in Mr. White's absence, the information you
require.

    I have enclosed details, such as they are, on how to become involved with
the annual "Song for Europe" extravaganza which is the exercise all British
songwriters must experience before rising to the heights of the international
contest. However, my impression is, and in mentioning this I do not wish to
insult Viola's Goldfish, albeit lyrical, neither do I intend to rob Roger of his
finest, nay, brightest hour in his gold lamé (what impeccable taste Reginald's
late wife must have had!) but have you ever thought of allowing the European
Common Market to benefit from your extremely eloquent pen? Forget the cos lettuce, (sorry Roger), the home made jams, pasties, and yes, even the Eurovision
Song Contest, and give the world what you gave us, words that were a pleasure
for our eyes to behold and our intellects digest. You are aiming too low by
encouraging the youngsters in tight trousers and short skirts, whether male or
female (and who can tell these days?); your talent should be aimed at more ele-
vated targets.

    Whatever you decide, I am sure that you will think of England and when you
stand up to be counted at the end, your score will be the highest at "douze
points".

                         Yours sincerely

                         JANICE CABLE (Mrs.)
                         Assistant to the Secretary

REGISTERED IN LONDON NUMBER 140248 REGISTERED OFFICE 103 KINGSWAY LONDON WC2B 6QX to find Jamaican half-crowns in your change, and how much more annoying it would be for us to labour hard all day at this Common Market and return home only to find that we had a pocketful of bottle-tops taken, in good faith, as these European currency units.

Roger returns from his latest fishing expedition with one small eel. Embarrassed by his lack of success, he blames over-fishing by other members of the Common Market, especially (so he says) a Dutchman who was further along the pier using two rods and who caught six fish. I do not think this is quite the right time to show him a letter that arrived in the second post from Admiral Sir James Eberle. Anxious to avoid just this sort of plundering of our waters by foreign fishermen, I approached Sir James to see if he could undertake the policing of our stretch of channel west of the Admiralty Pier, Dover. Given his twin qualifications, as a navy man and an expert in international affairs, he would have been ideal. If, for example, he were to catch a French trawler (or indeed an over-zealous Dutchman with too many rods) making off with fish which were, under Common Market rules, rightfully ours, then he would be able to give them chapter and verse on the regulations. I explained to Sir James that it would help if he had his own small craft enabling him to engage in 'hot pursuit' of any miscreants, but if he did not, and could not borrow one from the Royal Navy, I would have a word with Mr Dennis, a friend of Mr Oliver's, whose leisure park was recently made bankrupt, to see if he could loan us something from the watersplash of the Fairy Grotto. Unfortunately Sir James is not able to help us, but it was a kind thought of his to pass on our concern to the Royal Navy.

Thursday, 17 May

Work progresses steadily on the plans for our Euro-summit here at 3 Cherry Drive. I have begun drawing up a list of the subjects that I think should be discussed, and have quite deliberately steered the agenda round to a subsidy for our lupins before lunch on day one. With the prospect of both barbecued pork sausages and home-made coleslaw, followed by Gâteau Odette, awaiting them, I feel that progress through this last item will be swift and, hopefully, to our advantage. Roger has dubbed this little gathering the Lupin Talks, or 'les discours de lupin'. One point does however cause me concern, that of security. I have asked Mr Bridger to cast his practised military eye over our arrangements. As far as I know there are no international terrorists resident in Canterbury, but as Mr Bridger says, it is better to be safe than sorry, and we should remember Sarajevo. I nod sagely, feeling embarrassed to admit I don't know who Sarajevo was or, indeed, what happened to him.

At Mr Bridger's suggestion I have instructed Roger to paint a large white H on the lawn. I am not entirely happy with this exercise, for I suspect it will take some years of growth and re-seeding to restore the pristine beauty of the grass, but such action is apparently necessary to ensure the safe landing of the helicopters bringing the heads of government. For much the same reason Mr Bridger has trimmed one side of the Bramley, giving it a most lopsided and unsteady look. He then insists that we test his security precautions by lying in wait and trapping Roger, who is due back soon from having the wax removed from his ears. After two hours of crouching with my back aching badly, I am surprised to find the odour of bacon and onions coming from the kitchen. It appears that while Mr Bridger and I were watching the routes of entry down the side of the house, Roger let himself in by the front door. It was a very embarrassed Mr Bridger who tried to explain away his mistake by saying that any terrorists were unlikely to have a latch-key. But if we are to play host to so many heads of government, such lapses will not do.

I have therefore decided that we must engage a professional, and to that end have approached Sir Robert Mark who, I understand, was quite high up in the police force before he retired and went into advertising. Sir Robert will undoubtedly have a great deal of experience in such matters, and I have

The Royal Institute of International Affairs

Chatham House 10 St James's Square London SW1Y 4LE
Telephone 01 930 2233 Cables Areopagus London

Patron Her Majesty the Queen

From: Admiral Sir James Eberle GCB

10 May 1984

Mr W Morgan Petty
3 Cherry Drive
Canterbury
Kent

Dear Mr Morgan Petty,

Thank you for your letter of 30 April. I
feel sure that the Royal Navy is entirely capable
of policing all our UK waters. I will pass on
your concern over the area to the West of the
Admiralty Pier, Dover to the appropriate Naval
Authority.

Yours sincerely,

Caroline Adams
PP Sir James Eberle

(Dictated by Sir James Eberle
and signed in his absence)

asked if he could take on the role of security chief for the duration of the conference. I have also asked for some indication of his fee and explained that it would be helpful if he still had his uniform and could bring his own walkie-talkie and truncheon. It is only after I have posted the letter that I realize my error: we do not have a walkie-talkie, and if Sir Robert were only to bring the one then he would be left talking to himself.

Friday, 18 May

Two letters in the post this morning. The first is from Michael Butler. As the United Kingdom's Permanent Representative to the European Communities he is optimistic about the prospects for our products at the Common Market and goes on to say that the fisheries policy provides an excellent framework for U.K. fishermen. I am not entirely sure Roger would agree. The second letter is from Sir Hugh Casson at the Royal Academy of Arts. It seems that Sir Hugh is unable to help us in mounting our exhibition, which is a pity, as Roger is way behind schedule on the necessary construction work, having lost the head of his two-pound claw-hammer and being forced to knock in the six-inch nails with the camping mallet.

On the question of building work, I have felt from the very beginning that it is vitally important for us here at 3 Cherry Drive to have, as do the other members of the Common Market, our own internationally recognizable landmark, if only to put on our carrier bags. Like theirs, I feel that this should be a monument to the national character: the instability of the Italians reflected by the tower of Pisa, the state of the Greek economy indicated by the Parthenon or the dour nature of the Flems so succinctly summed up by that big silver thing in Brussels that looks like ball-bearings soldered together. After discussions with Roger and Ingrid I decide that we shall build a Euro-tower with a revolving vegetarian restaurant at the top. At first I had grave doubts about the

43

advisability of the restaurant, preferring instead just a little platform looking out over the countryside. However Ingrid, whose ideas both the restaurant and its vegetarian nature were, offers to help with its running and, more importantly, points out that, even with the expected grant aid from the Common Market, this is not going to be a cheap project to undertake, and income from the restaurant, should it prove to be a success, would be very helpful.

Despite Roger's evident enthusiasm, I decline his kind offer to design our Euro-tower. I think we must definitely have a professional. I do not relish, during periods of high winds and other inclement weather, lying awake worrying as to whether our Euro-tower has collapsed across the neighbouring gardens. I have therefore written to Colonel Richard Seifert, who I understand is a widely respected architect of tall buildings, having designed something called 'Centrepoint' which is much taller than our Euro-tower needs to be and has so far shown no signs of falling over. I just hope he is not too busy to help.

Saturday, 19 May

Thunder and lightning. Mr Bridger, who was caught in the downpour, sits steaming in the kitchen. Roger and myself, doing our best to ignore his repeated remark that 'we didn't have this sort of weather in May until we joined the Common Market,' sort through a pile of P.E. kit. Most of this has not seen the light of day for some considerable time, a fact made obvious by the legend on one yellowing vest: GOOD LUCK PHILIP AND ELIZABETH. I remember this garment being worn by the torch-bearer who lit the celebratory bonfire on the occasion of the present Queen's marriage to young Mr Mountbatten. Unfortunately it seems that Roger too has had an idea for cementing closer relations with the other countries of Europe, to wit participating in the European Games. I have my reservations, feeling that we may be taking on too much already. But since he has gone to all the trouble of

Foreign and Commonwealth Office

London SW1A 2AH

5 July 1984

W Morgan Petty Esq
3 Cherry Drive
CANTERBURY
Kent

Dear Mr Petty,

    Mr Rifkind was delighted for the confirmation in your
letter of 3 July that you and Roger have taken over
responsibility for your own dealings with the European
Community. It is a weight off our minds. You will find
we have done some of the spade-work on your behalf over the
past decade as a consequence of which 3 Cherry Drive is your
 'vacant pitch' and the inhabitants of the Community are
your market. All 270 million - with the possible exception
of Sacha Distel - will, I doubt not, beat a path to your Cos
lettuces and to Viola's legs.

    If you do decide to expand into pasties, remember to
call them 20% meat comestibles, and list the various protein
binders for which the Odette Sisters are so justly famous.

    The British, I agree, produce the finest 'Euro artistes'.
Stick to them.

    As to grants, there may well be rich pickings to be had.
Now that you have taken over direct dealings, I suggest you make
it one of your first tasks to identify them.

                    yours etc

                    Anthony Cary

                    Anthony Cary
                    Private Secretary to
                    Malcolm Rifkind

ROYAL ACADEMY OF ARTS,
PICCADILLY, LONDON, W1V 0DS

Telephone: 01-734 9052
Cables: Royacad, London

15th May 1984

Dear Mr Petty

    Forgive my long delay in replying to your letter of 18th April - due to pressure of work in mounting our Summer Exhibition.

    Forgive, too, my inability to come to the aid of your Common Market proposal. So sorry and good luck.

Sir Hugh Casson
President

W. Morgan Petty, Esq.,
3 Cherry Drive,
Canterbury,
Kent.

bringing this P.E. kit down from the attic I feel obliged to write to the President of the Amateur Athletics Association and make some inquiries. I explain that I am a little long in the tooth for participation in these games (unless whist is included), although I am proud to let them know that I won a silver cup for hop, step and jump at junior school. Any hope for a medal for Cherry Drive must lie with Roger, who once took second place in a fifty yards egg and spoon race. Is there, I ask them, such an event in these European Games? If so, I am sure he will not disgrace us. If not, then perhaps I could offer to help out on the administrative side, and I am sure Roger would be quite happy to blow up the mattresses for the high-jumpers to land on. Roger tries on the several pairs of black plimsolls that he has found, but of the only pair that fit the left one has no toe-cap. More expense. Secretly I hope that we are found in some way ineligible for participation in these games, not least because I have since discovered that we would have to parade around at the beginning with our national flag and, quite frankly, we do not have one.

Monday, 21 May

Excellent news. A letter from Sir Henry Plumb. After preliminary congratulations on our efforts he speculates that we are receiving a percentage of the rebates on the British contribution. Indeed we are not. Certainly if, as Sir Henry suggests, we should be, then I calculate that on his figure of one per cent we are due as income from this source some twenty-five million pounds. We could certainly afford to mend the shed roof then, or in fact go the whole hog and buy a new one. I am just mulling over how much we should spend of this new-found wealth and how much I should put in the building society when I am struck by the terrible thought that maybe cheques meant for us are being sent to the wrong address. I write straight away to the European Commission, asking that they make sure that any repayments due are sent directly here. Sir Henry also helps solve, if not entirely, the question of the Common Market's location. According to him this does not exist on the 'vulgarly physical plain'. Despite a search of my historical atlas I cannot find the 'vulgarly physical plain', which I suspect is, as its name implies, a bit like Salisbury Plain. Roger suggests that the name might have been changed, as he understands that quite a lot of re-naming went on in Europe after the Second World War. Well at least if, on our European travels, we see a sign to this 'vulgarly physical plain' we can carry straight on in the knowledge that the Common Market is not being held there.

Tuesday, 22 May

An extraordinary day, not least because it began with such excitement: Mr Oliver banging on the front door at six o'clock in the morning. He carries with him two suitcases and a box containing his photographic equipment and asks if he may stay for a few days 'until the heat is off'. Over several cups of black coffee the whole sordid story comes out. The tea-shop in Norwich was, as I had suspected, less than a success, and when he and Michael Hardiman agreed to dissolve their partnership 'for personal reasons' it was left to the latter to sell the fixtures and fittings, settle the outstanding debts and divide equally any remaining money. It now appears that Mr Oliver's erstwhile partner has decamped to the Costa del Sol with all the cash without first settling accounts, and that the broker's men are hard on Mr Oliver's heels. Looking at him sitting forlornly behind the kitchen table in crumpled blazer and green and orange striped shirt, I am moved by pity and promise that, if he agrees to help with the garden and reimburse us for any extra expense, he may stay. In reply he empties his pockets of what little money he has and goes for a lie down. I discover on examining the coins that they are quite a mixture, Italian lire, Spanish pesetas and Japanese yen. Tips from members of his tourist parties no doubt. Unfortunately in coin of our own realm there are but two new pence. I just hope I am doing the right thing.

Conservative and Unionist Party, GB
Det konservative folkeparti, DK
Ulster Unionist Party, N. Ireland

EUROPEAN DEMOCRATIC GROUP

EUROPEAN PARLIAMENT

Chairman

Sir Henry Plumb, DL, MEP

LONDON

2 Queen Anne's Gate
London, SW1H 9AA
Tel. (01)222 1720
(01)222 1729
Telex 917650 EDGLDN

17th May, 1984

Dear Mr. Morgan Petty,

Thank you for your letter of 8th April. I am sorry that it has only just been delivered to me from Luxembourg.

I should like to congratulate you most sincerely on your appointment as intermediary between the UK and Europe. It is typical of the indifference the media display towards the Community that so little publicity has been given to your well deserved appointment, although I do seem to recall hearing a reference to it on Gardeners Question Time over Easter. I hope the Foreign Office's giving you this appointment is not another example of their tendency to wash their hands of unwanted colonial problems: after all, the other 9 countries of the Common Market applied to join us in 1973 and one cannot just abandon them because they do not understand the British way of doing things. I prefer to believe that your appointment is another example of the privatisation programme to which this Government is committed. I assume that your contract is on a commercial basis, and that you receive, say, 1% of the rebates from the British contribution to the Community which you negotiate with our partners (1% of £2,500 million over the last 5 years is not to be sneezed at!).

I must confess a certain embarrassment when you ask me about the dates and places on which the Common Market takes place. Our Common Market does not exist on a vulgarly physical plain, but is rather to be found in the hearts and minds of Europeans. The British Conservatives have long pressed for the realisation of the genuine internal market and an end to those barriers to trade within the Community which still exist. Once these barriers to trade have been abolished, you should find a ready market for your vegetables, jam and pastries. (I should perhaps warn you against expanding too recklessly in the jam and pastries market; I have inside information that these products are in structural surplus and that quotas are just around the corner).

Should you be passing through London on your next Euro jaunt, I should be happy if you would make yourself known to my office at the above address.

HENRY PLUMB

Mr. W. Morgan Petty,
3, Cherry Drive,
Canterbury,
Kent.

An item on the Home Service brings us the news that irate French dairy farmers have kidnapped the head of that country's Milk Marketing Board. Perhaps Dr Fitzgerald was wise in his decision not to make deliveries here. It would have been very embarrassing if the head of a friendly government were, while driving his milk cart through the streets of Canterbury, manhandled by a gang of these red-faced ruffians protesting about the imposition of something called 'milk quotas'. I am left once again to ponder over security for our own Lupin Talks. I have received a negative reply from the Dutch Prime Minister, Mr Lubbers, to my invitation, but that will still leave us with ten heads of Common Market countries (including myself) to protect. Furthermore I have had no reply from Sir Robert Mark, who Roger says may be away filming another tyre commercial. In his absence Roger has offered to do his best, but it will still be a daunting task. I have therefore asked Mr Heseltine, the Secretary of State for Defence, if there is a short course, run by the S.A.S., where after several weeks of training Roger might return, panther-like, fully equipped to storm buildings and rescue hostages. I am sure that Mr Heseltine will realize from our previous extensive correspondence that Roger is a willing pupil, and what is more he has his own black balaclava.

I discuss this possibility with Mr Bridger, who, anxious to redeem his own reputation after our last anti-terrorist exercise ended in such a fiasco, suggests that a further way to thwart potential assassins would be use of our own naturally-occurring foliage to block off avenues of fire. Unfortunately this thought came to him *after* he and Roger had heavily pruned both the privet and leylandii, and I fear there is little chance of these growing back before the talks. When I point this out there is a short, embarrassed silence followed by the further, hurried, suggestion that we overcome the problem by the use of 'instant trees'. I was not convinced at first that Mr Bridger was being entirely serious, but he insists he is, and explains

No.:344479.   The Hague, 21st May, 1984.

Dear Sir,

Thank you for your friendly letter of May 9th, 1984.
I am afraid I could not accept your invitation for
the gathering of political leaders, though it is an
innovative suggestion.

Yours sincerely,

R.M.F. Lubbers
Prime Minister.

To W. Morgan Petty
3, Cherry Drive
Canterbury, Kent
United Kingdom.

Postbus 20001 - 2500 EA 's-Gravenhage - Kantooradres: Binnenhof 20 - Tel. 070 - 61 40 31 that these are manufactured and used extensively by the Federal Bureau of Investigation for just such a purpose. Furthermore he tells me that hundreds of these instant trees are currently being erected in Ballyporeen in preparation for the visit of President Reagan to the birthplace of his ancestors. I seem to recall Roger mentioning such a visit, referring to it however in quite a different way as a 'cheap political stunt to win over the Irish vote' and saying even more unkindly, with reference to Mr Reagan's age, that he probably hadn't been back to the place since he left during the potato famine. On Mr Bridger's advice I drop a line to William H. Webster, the current Director of the F.B.I., asking for a catalogue of these instant trees and whether as well as the more mundane conifers they also do flowering and fruiting varieties.

Saturday, 26 May

Mr Oliver and Roger have had words. The acrimony began when our new guest commandeered the bathroom for more than an hour and used all the hot water. Roger, who had been forking over some particularly pungent compost (agitated with pig dung), was not at all pleased, a displeasure compounded by discovering that his 'friend' had cancelled the *Guardian* on our newspaper order, replacing it with the *Daily Mail* so that he might continue playing some sort of 'bingo'. I know that Roger sets great store by his status as a *Guardian* reader, regarding it as part of what he calls his 'life profile' – eating muesli, watching Channel Four, saving up to buy a Volvo, etc. – and when Mr Oliver refused his request to take the offending newspaper back and exchange it a struggle ensued during which both the newspaper and Roger's pullover were badly torn. He spends the rest of the morning sullenly planting his main-crop peas while Mr Oliver, in a violet kimono-style dressing-gown, occupies the settee in the lounge, eating cheese on toast and reading the fragments of newsprint.

Leaving this matter, hopefully, to cool, I reply to Colonel

Seifert's letter asking for more information about our Euro-tower. As he requests, I enclose a location drawing and tell him that I envisage our landmark as a cross between the Monument to the Great Fire of London and the Post Office Tower, thus incorporating the best elements of both the old and the new. I further explain that the base can be no more than eight feet in diameter (any larger and it would mean moving the hyacinths, which will not be at their best for at least two years). Given this limited space I suspect that a lift is out of the question and we shall have to make do with the sort of steps more normally found in medieval castles. Still, a climb up a hundred or two of these should give diners a keen appetite for the potage de lettuce, lettuce pancakes and lettuce à la Cherry Drive that Ingrid has promised to serve for at least the first month or so to help rid us of our embarrassing surplus of this salad vegetable.

Monday, 28 May

Plans proceed apace for the Lupin Talks. I must say that when I first envisaged holding this little get-together I expected the arrangements would be relatively simple. Roger would show everybody to their room and, once they had settled in, the heads of government and myself would spend the weekend enjoying a few glasses of elderflower wine and making the odd policy decision. It is certainly proving far more difficult, what Roger calls the 'logistical' aspects providing the biggest headache. For a start we share, with the bureaucracy in Brussels, a lack of seating. I am hoping that Mr Bridger's brother Arthur can help us out there with some deck-chairs, although how the heads of Common Market governments will feel about reposing in seats with a dubious history and the words PROPERTY OF MARGATE DISTRICT COUNCIL I am not sure.

The guiding principle behind making these arrangements is 'protocol', or doing things properly. Something which has to be done properly is the end-of-talks photograph, not only

R SEIFERT & PARTNERS

Chartered Architects

164 Shaftesbury Avenue London WC2H 8HZ

Telephone 01-242 1644
Cables Seiferts London WC2
Telex 296622 Sefrts G

Partners
R Seifert J P DIP ARCH (UCL) F R I B A
J M Seifert B Sc DIP ARCH (UCL) R I B A
                CROAIF (FR) NCARB Cert (USA)
H G Marsh F R I B A
A G Henderson DIP ARCH A R I B A
R F Morris B ARCH (UCD) A R I B A
R J Jenkins B A R I B A
S Alexander B ARCH DIP TP A R I B A
H E Morgan A R I B A
J Clowes DIP ARCH A R I B A
L H Watson R I B A A R I A S

our ref   RS/MW   your ref   date   22nd May, 1984

Dear Mr. Morgan Petty,

I have read your letter of the 17th May, 1984 with interest,
but I find it difficult to fully understand what exactly is
required.

If you would be good enough to enlarge upon the matter and
provide me with a location drawing, I will let you know the
fee which I would require.

Yours sincerely,

W. Morgan Petty, Esq.,
3, Cherry Drive,
Canterbury,
Kent.

Associates
P Milne DIP ARCH ARIBA W J Gander ARIBA MSIAD M R Byrne DIP ARCH ARIBA R Christie Gammie RIBA E Kural DIP ARCH ING (ITU) RIBA V Mayes DIP ARCH ARIBA
F T Johnson RIBA M J Elliott BSc DIP ARCH (UCL) RIBA L M Winter RIBA M F W Walshe BA AA DIP RIBA A Lynch DIP ARCH RIBA

Interior Design   Environmental Design   Landscape Architecture   Finance and Administration
G L Hook FSIAD   C W Green FCIBS C Eng MIMech E   S G Wardell DIP LA ALI   R P Reeves FAAI MInstCM MBIM

In Association with
R Seifert Co-Partnership Trafalgar House Hope Street Glasgow C2 Scotland Telephone 041 221 0232

to provide a nice souvenir for the participants but, according to Mr Bridger, vitally important as placing on record for members of the public the fact that no matter how violent the quarrels may have been behind closed doors, no one has blacked anyone else's eye. I was hoping Roger would take this snap, but he will almost certainly be too busy over the weekend of the talks, what with his responsibility for security and his promise to give a lecture and practical demonstration on dealing with brown root rot. I am sure that our guests will find this riveting, as I understand that it is a disease very common among the large pot plants so often found in government offices. Mr Oliver did offer to take the picture but, despite the fact that he has a new automatic wide-angle lens, I refused, as my hope is that he will be gone long before the talks take place.

I have therefore decided to ask the Earl of Lichfield, or Patrick, as I understand he prefers being called, if he will undertake the commission. I wondered if we could afford his lordship, but Roger points out that we might make a saving if 'Patrick' takes the pictures and he pops the negatives along to Boot's for printing. It is strange, I had always rather thought of earls as sitting grandly in their clubs waiting for servants to bring them freshly ironed copies of *The Times*, but, according to Roger, 'Patrick' is not at all like this. I ask his lordship whether he is familiar with Roger's work. If he takes *The Kentish Camera Club Quarterly*, he could not fail to have noticed 'Unusual Aspects of Mistletoe', which won third place in the Christmas competition and was reproduced in full colour on the centre pages. It later turns out that I have already seen Lord Lichfield in television commercials demonstrating cameras, but I naturally thought he was an actor. After all, you don't expect the Milk Tray man to jump on train roofs on his way to work or spend his evenings off swimming through shark-infested waters. One thing however does bother me. Roger has also told me Patrick's speciality is photographing people with their clothes off, for calendars, and I am not sure it would be altogether to their taste or consistent with 'protocol' if Europe's political leaders were to appear in the buff above the month of August.

Wednesday, 30 May

Mr Oliver has eaten all the bacon. I had been saving three rashers for our tea. Not only that but he used the last of the milk and left the washing-up in the sink. More seriously, I suspect that he was the individual responsible for writing something very rude on the bottom of Ingrid's banner depicting Mrs Pankhurst, the suffragette leader. For some reason this embellishment went unnoticed until she and her 'sisters in solidarity' had carried it aloft for some hours while 'reclaiming the night' in Market Harborough. What is more, I further suspect that he has been reading items of my correspondence. Yesterday he was very inquisitive about 'fact-finding' trips undertaken by members of the Common Market and subsidized by that organization. I confess that at first I was rather flattered that he seemed genuinely interested in our European progress, but all illusion was shattered when he asked if I could use my influence to 'wangle him on one of those to Barbados or Grand Bahama'. Taken aback, I inquired just what sort of facts he expected to find there, to which he replied that he did not know but, given two or three weeks of sunshine and rum punch, he was sure he would come up with something. I find it too much of a coincidence that only hours before I had written to the Commission urging them to fund a visit, by Roger, to the Netherlands for the purpose of studying tomato irrigation, and had left the letter on the living-room table, unsealed, prior to posting. Enough is enough, and I resolve to tackle him. When I raise the subject of the bacon he interrupts and tells me that I do not need to apologize that there were ONLY three slices because he knows how busy I am and how little time I have to go to the shops. Furthermore he makes no secret of the fact that he read my letter, saying he had finished his library book. While I stand speechless he exits with the excuse that he is in a hurry to cash

56

a cheque before the bank closes. I am still a little stunned when Roger comes in and angrily complains that someone has left a piece of bacon rind between the pages of his current reading matter, *The Female Eunuch*. Ingrid's suggestion no doubt. I notice that this too is a library book, but feel it is better to say nothing in the circumstances.

Friday, 1 June

The post brings a helpful reply from Mr George Scott at the Commission of the European Communities (which I recently discovered was the full and posher name for the Market authority). I wrote to him on the advice of Mr Christopher Tugendhat with yet another, and hopefully more successful, grant request, this time for the funding of a weekend course in grafting fruit-trees. I know for a fact that in this part of the country there is great resentment at the importation of large quantities of French apples: Mr Bridger's one-man protest outside the greengrocer's, made more boisterous by recent attendance at a real ale festival, almost resulted in his arrest for disorderly conduct. I therefore thought that we could, using our expertise, cross both French and British varieties and solve the problem, creating an *entente* Granny Smith *et* Golden Delicious – a sort of Granny Delicious. Such is the way of bureaucracy that Mr Scott refers us on to yet another Common Market body, the European Parliament. As he suggests, I drop them a line in the hope that this, my second letter, will prove more productive than the first. On that occasion I asked how many seats had been allocated, in this Parliament, to us at 3 Cherry Drive, and I am sorry to say that I am still waiting for the reply. Maybe it has gone astray in the post. I suppose things will be cleared up after the European elections on June the ninth.

Our own arrangements for this election are proceeding well. Roger has painted up an old biscuit tin and stencilled the words BALLOT BOX along the top. I thought it prudent, in case Roger and myself were not allocated a seat each in this

Commission of the European Communities

8 Storey's Gate, London SW1P 3AT

Telephone: 01-222 8122   Telex: 23208 EUR.UK.G.

21 June 1984

Mr. W. Morgan Petty
3 Cherry Drive
Canterbury
Kent

Dear Mr. Petty,

Thank you for your letter of 12 June and the statistical annex. I agree that Roger made a first class job of it!

I have passed your suggestions on to Mr. George Clarke, who is the adviser to the Director General of the Statistical Office of the European Communities in Luxembourg and who happens to be a good friend of mine. Undoubtedly, he will contact you in due course.

In the meantime, I hope your efforts will bear fruit, and we would be only too pleased to receive samples of the jam and pasties, home made by the Odette Sisters, for tasting.

With kind regards.

Yours sincerely,

Marijke Maas (Miss)
Publications Department

Copy: George Clarke / Eurostat-Luxembourg

Cardiff Office:	Belfast Office:	Edinburgh Office:
4 Cathedral Road	Windsor House	7 Alva Street
Cardiff CF1 9SG	9/15 Bedford Street	Edinburgh EH2 4PH
Telephone: 0222-371631	Belfast N. Ireland	Telephone: 031-225 2058
	Telephone: 0232-240708	

Parliament, that we should only elect one M.E.P. to represent us. I originally thought that I would be the only candidate for this seat, but at the close of nominations I find that Roger has also 'thrown his hat into the ring', as I believe they say in political circles. He explains that in the interests of democracy the electorate (him and myself) should have a choice of candidates. Naturally I agree, although, putting aside false modesty, I do not think that I should be overly anxious about the result.

Saturday, 2 June

Two cryptic and disappointing replies concerning our Euro-tower. The first is from Lord McAlpine. I approached him with a view to his helping us build the thing. Roger, confident as always, was convinced that, armed with Colonel Seifert's plans, he could manage on his own, but I have my doubts whether this is a one-man job, and he would certainly need a bigger ladder. Naturally I would not expect his lordship to mix the concrete or lay the bricks himself. Despite Patrick Lichfield's example of combining membership of the Upper House with manual labour, I am sure that Lord McAlpine will have given this up long ago. Furthermore there is the question of his robes. Letitia Odette says that it is practically impossible to get brick-dust out of ermine. I saw his lordship's role more as assisting me with organization and administration and knowing, from his vast experience, where we could hire the services of six burly navvies and a big crane most cheaply. It is to the question of cost that the second missive refers. The Chairman of the Abbey National Building Society, Sir Campbell Adamson, has written declining my request for a mortgage. In the circumstances I can only hope that the European Investment Bank, whom I have also approached for financial assistance, will be more forthcoming.

59

Monday, 4 June

Electioneering for our seat in the European parliament begins in earnest. Roger, clipboard in hand, arrives at the front door for some early canvassing. He asks whether I am prepared to reveal my voting intentions. Just to add a little mystery to the proceedings I declare myself a 'don't know'. He spends a further few minutes trying to persuade me to cast my vote for him and leaves a poster with the words ROGER FOR EUROPE written across it in green crayon. For my part I hold a public meeting this evening in the living room, where I address the voter (Roger) on the plans I have for Cherry Drive when it is fully integrated into Common Market membership. At the end of the meeting he gives me a rousing round of applause and takes my poster reading VOTE PETTY THE CHARLE-MAGNE OF TOMORROW which he promises to put in the window of the garden shed where we can both see it. Mr Oliver, who still shows no sign of leaving, voiced the opinion that he too should have a vote in the election, an idea I hurriedly countered by inventing a minimum residential qualification of two years. I was quietly congratulating myself on quick thinking when Mr Oliver laughed and said that in that case it would have to wait until next time. I do so hope it was a joke.

Tuesday, 5 June

I have made a decision. According to the *Daily Mail* newspaper, delivered again this morning and still the source of constant friction between Mr Oliver and Roger, there is to be a meeting of the heads of European governments later this month at somewhere called Fontainebleau. I express surprise that I have not yet received my invitation, but Roger says that they are probably late in sending them out. Just in case of any further delay, I send off a postcard to Monsieur Mitterrand, who I understand is organizing this, announcing my intention to attend. I decide not to raise the question of

SIR CAMPBELL ADAMSON
CHAIRMAN

ABBEY NATIONAL BUILDING SOCIETY,
27 BAKER STREET,
LONDON, WIM 2AA
TELEPHONE: 01-486 5544

25th May 1984

W. Morgan Petty Esq.,
3 Cherry Drive,
CANTERBURY,
Kent.

Dear Mr. Petty,

Thank you for your letter of May 22nd
and I hope that your enterprise will flourish.

Alas, Abbey National is not able to help
you with your project as this is outside the
area we deal with.

Yours sincerely,

Patricia Linden

(c.vs)

CAMPBELL ADAMSON

Dictated by Sir Campbell and signed in his
absence.

lupins at Fontainebleau, preferring to save this for home ground, but I am sure the experience will prove very instructive for the holding of our own event. It occurs to me that Fontainebleau must be where Monsieur Mitterrand lives, in which case he may be experiencing similar organizational problems to ourselves, especially over seating. Should I, I wonder, pack a couple of deck-chairs just to be on the safe side? I shall see how much room there is left on the roof-rack.

While Roger is out Ingrid arrives with a cardboard box. It seems that she has managed to find some plaster moulds of feminist figures after all – not her first choice of suffragettes throwing themselves in front of Derby runners but of an ancient British queen, Boadicea of the Iceni, chopping up Roman soldiers (or, as Ingrid described them, 'lackeys of imperial patriarchy') with knives strapped to the wheels of her chariot. The cardboard box contains the first batch she has produced, about which she would like my opinion. I brace myself for a disaster similar to those Roger has experienced, but am surprised to find that they are perfect in every detail, even down to the nought with a cross on it that Ingrid and her friends all have embroidered on their jumpers, and which has been painted on to Queen Boadicea's helmet. I congratulate her on her success and tell her that I am sure Roger will be pleased. If only I were.

Thursday, 7 June

This morning I do not find Roger, as instructed, weeding the onion bed and suspect that he is instead sulking in the shed. (Ingrid's second batch of plaster ornaments was equally successful, and I have allowed her, much to his annoyance, to keep these in the box room.) You can therefore imagine my surprise when I pushed back the shed door expecting to see a very sullen garden helper only to find him happily engrossed in a volume entitled *Australian Mammals* which he says he is reading in preparation for the arrival of our Euro-kangaroo. I must say I think he is being a little premature –

after all, we are not yet certain that a kangaroo-keeping subsidy is available to members of the Common Market. We only have Letitia Odette's claim that she heard something to this effect on the Home Service. Given that her hearing is not what it once was, and that she admits to turning the radio on midway through this item, the evidence is hardly conclusive. Her recollection is that, as its name implies, the Kangaroo Group has been set up to encourage the keeping of these creatures within the borders of Common Market countries. Roger, always keen on wildlife (I remember the time he nursed a hedgehog, injured in a road accident, back to a complete recovery), has rather seized on this and insists I find out all the details. I do so reluctantly, for, while I am sure he would be a most attentive keeper of what I understand the Australians call a 'joey', he does have rather a lot of other things to keep him busy at present.

In the post comes a letter from Dr David Owen. It is somewhat cryptic, but Roger speculates that Dr Owen will want to consider fully the implications of negotiating such things as an artificial ski-slope on our behalf. At least it is not a definite no. I wonder, if he eventually agrees to act for us, whether Dr Owen would also like to undertake the negotiations and get the best deal on the kangaroo?

Friday, 8 June

Roger is holding his election meeting outdoors this evening as the weather is fine. In preparation he has strung a banner between the russet and Beauty of Bath apple-trees. Sadly pressed for time, and against my advice, he left the painting of the slogan to Ingrid, who in turn delegated the task to Jaz, and thus we the voters of 3 Cherry Drive, Canterbury, are being urged to ROFTH ERGOW GARORIDW. I have just given up trying to decipher what I am sure is a stirring message when Viola Odette appears, her face wreathed in smiles. It transpires that she has been working, in conditions of the utmost secrecy, to perfect a European cheese. Her purpose in

63

THE RT HON DR DAVID OWEN MP

HOUSE OF COMMONS
LONDON SWIA OAA

30th May 1984

W Morgan Petty Esq
3 Cherry Drive
Canterbury
Kent

Dear Mr Petty

Thank you for your entertaining letter of
13th May.

I wish you well.

Yours sincerely,

<u>David Owen</u>

developing 'Le Fromage européen', she tells us, was twofold: as a gesture of friendship to our Common Market partners, and, if it catches on in a big way, to generate much-needed cash. Like all the great chefs, Viola is reticent on the subject of the recipe, but does confide in me that the cheese is European in content as well as spirit, with at least one ingredient from each of the eleven members of the Market including ourselves: blood sausage from Germany, raw herring from the Netherlands, garlic from Italy, etc. As we are all together, Viola suggests a grand tasting. Frankly this was not a great success, and the collective opinion was that although it was a very pretty colour (pink, due to the blood sausage), the taste was, to put it quite bluntly, appalling. Still, in true Community spirit, and not wishing to hurt Viola's feelings, we all ate up and did our best to smile. This brief experience drove any thought of marketing 'Le Fromage européen' from my mind. However Roger, despite the funny colour of his complexion, insists that we should not abandon the idea altogether and that it is just a matter of getting people used to the taste. Maybe, as he says, we do owe it to the Community to see that our cheese is a success, and what is more he puts forward the far more persuasive argument that we could badly do with the cash. I have therefore dropped a line to Sir Stephen Roberts, Chairman of the Milk Marketing Board, asking for a few hints on how we may turn our European cheese into an international favourite. At seven-thirty, despite a persistent feeling of queasiness, I take my seat at Roger's meeting. I am saddened to learn, from a note pinned to a tree, that the candidate is indisposed and will not be speaking after all.

Saturday, 9 June

Up six times in the night, and the morning finds me stricken with stomach pains. This on a day with so much to do. I decide to leave a list of jobs for Roger and retire once again to my bed. However the view of his own ashen features as he stumbles into a kitchen chair rules this possibility out. He informs me that he too had a disturbed night – visits to the lavatory interspersed with dreams of being devoured by a giant herring. What, he asks weakly pouring himself a cup of tea, would Freud make of it? Suspecting that Freud is one of his friends from the Camera Club, and having never made his acquaintance, I really do not know. With our both feeling nauseous, I decide that we should spend the day on paperwork for 'le discours de lupin'.

There are a number of immediate problems that need solving. The first is one of transport. I am surprised to learn that it is protocol to carry the heads of government from the helicopter landing site (behind the gladioli) to the patio by means of a bullet-proof car. As this is only a distance of some thirty feet I think they should be able to walk, but if it is the done thing, then do it we must. Roger suggests that we create an immediately favourable impression on our guests by using an armour-plated Rolls-Royce. While I have no doubt that in purchasing such a vehicle we would be getting the very best, the question is, can we afford it? I have dropped a line to Sir Richard Cave, Chairman of Rolls-Royce Motors, asking about the cost of a model with this bullet-proof facility. It may well be that they have one tucked away at the back of their showroom which was ordered by the Prime Minister or President of some politically unstable country who was overthrown and shot before he could take delivery. If so, maybe they would consider letting us have this at a discount.

A second difficulty concerns the actual talks themselves. I have already invited Sir Nicholas Henderson, the former British ambassador to the United Nations, asking if he would take the chair. I am not expecting any great acrimony and had thought myself capable of sorting out any minor disputes but, according to Mr Bridger, this is not possible, as I must be seen to be as Caesar's wife. I do not think he was being rude. I am sure that Sir Nicholas will make an excellent referee, knowing from his vast experience at the U.N. when, in political terms, 'to blow the whistle and show the yellow card' to our eminent guests.

On the question of strategy at the talks, I am wondering how best to approach the subject of our subsidy. Should I take the more lupin-minded heads of government aside and build an alliance, or should I simply spell out the position and depend on the good sense of our European partners for its success? I am inclined to agree with Roger that the latter course stands very little chance, and for that reason I should consider the former. I must confess unfamiliarity with the sort of wheeling and dealing, in smoke-filled rooms, that may be necessary to obtain our lupin subsidy, and so I have approached the Right Honourable Francis Pym, who (it appears) is, like Dr David Owen, a former Foreign Secretary. (There certainly do seem to be a lot of them about.) I have asked Mr Pym if he will act as our adviser at the forthcoming talks, explaining that even if he is ignorant on the subject of lupins it does not matter as Roger will fill him in on the details, and that what we would want from him is advice on when to shout and bang the table, when to go off into the corner in a huff, and all the other little tricks of international diplomacy.

Tuesday, 12 June

Roger and myself venture into town to have the passport photographs that we will need to travel to Fontainebleau taken by the machine in the bus station. I cannot say they are good likenesses. My own features resemble those of Lawrence Tierney in the film *Dillinger*, and Roger, who was caught unawares by the flashlight, has the appearance of someone discovered doing something he ought not to be. Still, at fifty pence for a sheet of four they will have to do. On our way back home we are stopped by a gentleman wearing a large blue rosette who asks if we shall be voting in the forthcoming European elections. When we answer in the affirmative he gives us some leaflets, and urges us to vote Conservative. I must say he seemed somewhat startled when Roger handed him in return a copy of his own manifesto, which by chance he had with him, explaining that neither of the candidates at 3 Cherry Drive was standing as a Conservative and that we both greatly valued our status as independents.

The brochure we have been given is most interesting, detailing as it does the location, surface area and population of the members of the European Community. There is however, I point out, just one thing wrong: the information provided makes no mention of ourselves. I thought nothing more of this, spending the rest of the day busily filling in the passport forms and pasting on the dubious reproductions of Roger and myself, and so it was a great surprise when at teatime Roger presented me with his afternoon's work: a copy of the leaflet so amended as to include our own details. I must say he has made a first-class job of it, and so pleased am I that I shall send a copy to the publications department of the Commission who, I have no doubt, will be only too happy to use it and be saved the trouble of redrawing the information themselves.

Thursday, 14 June

Election day. Along with all the other members of the Common Market, except for some strange reason Great Britain, we have adopted the single transferable vote system. When the polling station opens, a little late because Mr Bridger, who is acting as clerk but does not share our enthusiasm for Europe, forgot the date, I fill in my ballot paper. Naturally I am my first choice and put Roger second. I had expected the other candidate to be similarly fast off the mark but learn that, suffering a cheese-poisoning relapse, he will not be voting until the afternoon – something which does not please Mr Bridger, who will have to sit at the trestle table in the garden until then.

In the post there are two letters. The first is from the Prado in Madrid. I know that Spain is not yet a member of the Common Market, but I thought it would be a nice gesture to

THE EUROPEAN COMMUNITY

Surface area (1000 km²)

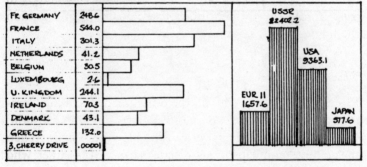

FR GERMANY	248.6
FRANCE	544.0
ITALY	301.3
NETHERLANDS	41.2
BELGIUM	30.5
LUXEMBOURG	2.6
U. KINGDOM	244.1
IRELAND	70.3
DENMARK	43.1
GREECE	132.0
3, CHERRY DRIVE	.0001

EUR 11
1657.6

USSR
22402.2

USA
9363.1

JAPAN
377.6

Population (x 1000)   Density per km²

Country	Population (x 1000)	Density per km²
FR GERMANY	61359	247
FRANCE	63480	98
ITALY	56014	189
NETHERLANDS	14039	341
BELGIUM	9848	823
LUXEMBOURG	364	140
U. KINGDOM	55946	229
IRELAND	3368	48
DENMARK	5117	119
GREECE	9449	71
3, CHERRY DRIVE	.0001	
EUR 11	269884	163
USSR	264108	12
USA	220584	24
JAPAN	115870	307

invite the premier museum of that country, a new boy like ourselves so to speak, to send a few pictures for our European art exhibition. Unfortunately they are unable to oblige, which I suspect may have something to do with not wishing to tempt fate over their membership application. The second and more positive response is from B.B.C. Television News. It is gratifying to note their enthusiasm for covering the Lupin Talks, though how we shall provide 100 three-pin plug sockets heaven only knows. Roger has voted. Now we must wait, along with the rest of Europe, until Sunday, when the ballot boxes are opened and the counting takes place, to find out who shall have the honour of representing us here at 3 Cherry Drive in the European Parliament.

Saturday, 16 June

Tension continues to mount as we wait for tomorrow's result, an atmosphere which occasions more sharp words between Mr Oliver and Roger. I do not think that in normal circumstances Roger would have lost his temper quite so badly if our 'paying guest', as Mr Oliver has taken to calling himself, had borrowed his electric razor to trim the loose ends from his suede shoes. While Mr Oliver lounges in front of the television watching *Play School*, I seek to find Roger some diversion before the situation becomes worse and blows are exchanged. My first thought, that he should spray the raspberries for cane blight, is thwarted by the onset of rain. It is then that I am struck by a brilliant idea. Some time after I first entered the realm of political self-sufficiency by declaring 3 Cherry Drive, Canterbury, a nuclear free zone I contacted the General Post Office with a view to their issuing a stamp to celebrate the event. Unfortunately they replied that, due to the considerable number of requests of this nature that they received, their policy was only to issue such stamps in commemoration of events in multiples of fifty years. This is certainly a long time to wait, and even if I should live to such an historic age, Roger and myself were not entirely sure that, given the present international situation, there would be anybody left to send letters to.

However, the matter of commemorative issues has grown more urgent of late with our membership of the Common Market. I understand that the other members are prolific in the issuing of such stamps, and we would certainly not wish to be outdone. I have therefore approached Sir Ronald Dearing at the General Post Office again with a proposal that we mark the milestones here at 3 Cherry Drive – the thousandth cos lettuce sold, gold medal for pastie-making, etc. – by issuing, under licence, our own commemorative stamps. (I know for a fact that Roger has an old Adana printing machine hidden under some sacking in the shed.) As yet I have not received Sir Ron's reply but, as I am sure they will be grateful for the extra business, have no doubt that it will be in the affirmative. I therefore ask Roger, who has an O-level in art, to design the first of these stamps, explaining that in my view this should be to celebrate our foray across the Channel to the Fontainebleau summit. I am pleased to say that he was most eager to accept the challenge, and the afternoon finds him at the easel, copy-sketching, from a volume entitled *The World Book of Wild Birds*, the Australian golah which he has chosen to adorn the first-class stamp.

One problem however remains. Whose profile, he asks, should be put in the corner? Obviously were we to follow the G.P.O.'s example of using Her Majesty the Queen there could be confusion between our stamps and theirs. I was just about, rather immodestly, to suggest my own visage when Ingrid arrived with a sack. She is, so she tells us, gathering items for a jumble sale to help pay Jaz's legal costs. On further inquiry it seems that her friend, while out protesting against male violence, put two policemen, who attempted to arrest her, into hospital, and now faces charges of assault. I agree to let her have a couple of old cardigans, and Roger, after some prompting, parts with his second-best garden hoe. While I am rummaging around upstairs in search of these ancient woollies Roger explains to Ingrid all about our commemorat-

MUSEO DEL PRADO
El Subdirector

Madrid, 11 de Junio de 1984

Mrs. W. Morgan Petty
3, Cherry Drive
Canterbury, Kent
GRAN BRETAÑA

Dear Mrs. Morgan Petty,

The Director is passing me your letter of May 4.

It is very interesting all the information about your activities, specially
of the Odette Sisters and Rogers.

It is a pity that Spain is not a member of the Common Market as you say, and
believe me, this is not a reason not to cooperating with you. But the policy
for loans at our Museum is very restrictive and the Trustees never agree
to loans unless they are for Museum of the same quality and importance of
the Prado. By the way El Greco was born in Greece, that's why he was called
El Greco, when he decided to live for the rest of his life in Spain. Probably
you can understand that, as there are many of your countrymen who also have
chosen to live in Spain for the rest of their lives, probably because of the
sun, for example Sir Robert Graves!.

With best regards.

Yours sincerely,

Manuela Mena

BBC TELEVISION NEWS
Television Centre · Wood Lane · London W12 7RJ · Telephone 01-743 8000

12 June 1984

Dear Mr. Morgan Petty,

      Thank you for your thoughtful letter of May 30.

      BBC Television News will certainly attend this major event at 3 Cherry Drive, Canterbury just as soon as you can give us the precise date and time.

      Naturally we would love it to be 'exclusive' but we are in your hands.

                     Yours sincerely,

                      Peter Woon
                        Editor
              BBC Television News

P.S. As normal we would require 100 three-pin plug sockets but no doubt you will find a way of providing them.

Mr. W. Morgan Petty,
3 Cherry Drive,
Canterbury,
KENT.

ive stamps, and on my return I find her insistent that any such corner profile should be female. Furthermore she says that, in keeping with the antipodean theme, we should use the head of her Australian idol Ms Germaine Greer. Against such enthusiasm for another any further suggestion of my own profile would have been embarrassing, and so I have written to Ms Greer asking both for her permission and a photograph.

Sunday, 17 June

Betrayal.

At precisely eleven o'clock, the time designated for the opening of the ballot boxes, and with everyone present, Mr Bridger, acting as returning officer, peeled off the string and sealing-wax, undid the padlock, and emptied out the voting slips. With a solemnity matching the occasion he announced the result. Roger and myself had one vote each and one second preference. Knowing who I voted for I thought Roger's actions dubious, although as it was a secret ballot I was constrained from voicing my suspicions that he had not voted for me. However we are now left with the problem of who is to take our seat in the European Parliament. I saw little point in asking for a re-count, and after consultation with Mr Bridger, who was anxious to get away before the public houses had all closed, we decided to settle the matter by the toss of a coin. This measure seemed entirely acceptable to Roger until he called heads only to see it land as tails, whereupon he began to have grave doubts about its legality. I was just reflecting, with relief, that the time I had spent on my acceptance speech, some twenty pages, had not been wasted when everyone suddenly found excuses to leave, the Odette sisters due to the impending arrival of Viola's son Reginald with her grandson and granddaughter, Wayne and Cheryl, Mr Bridger for urgent alcoholic refreshment, and Roger, in a deep sulk, still muttering about the unfairness of it all. Although I am sure that his misgivings are occasioned by nothing more than sour grapes, it would, I suppose, be as well to check. After all, I do not want the embarrassment of turning up at the European Parliament, briefcase neatly packed, pencils sharpened, ready to take my seat only to find that an electoral irregularity prevents me from doing so. I shall therefore drop a line to that nice Mr Seamus Burke, the Chief Executive of the Electoral Reform Society, to ask him, as an expert on elections, whether our toss of a coin is valid.

Mr Oliver is in the kitchen. Smirking, he tells me that had he had a vote he would most certainly have cast it for me. I notice that he has taken from the refrigerator, and spread on his water biscuits, the last of Viola's Euro-cheese. I was about to make him aware of this fact but decided that he would probably benefit from the experience and, as he was so keen to vote for me, one good turn deserved another.

Monday, 18 June

In the post this morning are two letters. The first is from Sir William Rees-Mogg at the Arts Council. Sadly they are unable to help in the financing of our European art exhibition. However Sir William does suggest that we confine the project to the work of living artists and have them pay their own expenses – corrugated cardboard, brown paper, string, etc. It is easy to see why such a far-sighted man has been given the task of overseeing the arts. With Roger's help I draw up a list of likely participants, including Sir Henry Moore, Marc Chagall and Pablo Picasso, and write offering them the chance to exhibit. It may well be the case that they have works which have been, in the parlance of the art world, 'difficult to shift'. I explain that if that is the case, we have no objection to their putting a little card in the corner with the price on. It may well be that among the crowds we expect to attend they will find a buyer. However if this is the case then Roger, himself an artist and with first-hand knowledge of such matters, says we should make it clear that we expect the usual percentage. I have also advised the artists to send the pictures by registered

76

delivery, as it would be a great shame if they were to go astray in the post.

The second letter is from 10 Downing Street and says that our 'proposals have been noted'. I accept without question that Mrs Thatcher is very busy; it was only yesterday that Mr Bridger told me she was trying to give Hong Kong back to the Chinese (if the poor quality of Roger's cassette recorder, made in that city, is any yardstick, then I can only hope that among the billions in the Land of the Dragon there are large numbers of people skilled in the repair of domestic electrical appliances). However, I was hoping that she would have been more positive in her reply to our invitation. It would cause great confusion if we were to allocate her single room to Monsieur Mitterrand, who it seems smokes those very smelly French cigarettes, only to have her turn up with her suitcase later. As well as being very busy, Mrs Thatcher is a very forceful woman, and I do not see her taking kindly to sleeping in a curtained-off corner of the room occupied by the West German Chancellor. This evening Roger, rather shamefaced, explains that Mr Picasso is dead, but that we shouldn't worry as works of deceased painters fetch higher prices which should increase our commission. I point out that this may well be the case, but who is to pay the postage on sending us the pictures in the first place?

Tuesday, 19 June

Mr Oliver is still ill. Roger, rather cruelly I thought, asked if he would like some bread and cheese for lunch, an invitation which caused the invalid to flee into the bathroom, where at the time of writing, several hours later, he remains. The good thing is that it has kept him out of the way while we prepare the plans for our journey to Fontainebleau. Roger is very keen to make it a round trip including, on our return, a visit to the city of Brussels where he says that I, fresh from the European summit, can take my seat in parliament while he attempts to climb the Butter Mountain. Frankly I must admit that I had

77

Arts Council of Great Britain 105 Piccadilly London W1V 0AU Telephone 01-629 9495 Telemessages Amec London W1

13 June 1984

W Morgan Petty, Esq
3 Cherry Drive
Canterbury
Kent

Dear Mr Petty,

Thank you very much for your letter of 21 May. I was interested to learn
of your enterprise and much regret that we are not in a position to help.
If you confined your project to the work of living artists you could no
doubt expect them to pay their own postage and all other expenses in con-
nection with their participation. I believe this is normally what is
expected in such circumstances.

Yours sincerely,

Chairman

10 DOWNING STREET

14 June 1984

Dear Mr Petty

I am writing in reply to your letter
to Mr Ingham about the proposed "Market"
and to say that your proposals have been
noted.

Yours sincerely

Beth Frier

BETH FRIER
PRESS OFFICE

W Morgan Petty Esq
3 Cherry Drive
CANTERBURY
Kent

never thought of Brussels as a city with mountains, although I have no first-hand knowledge – a situation which would have been very different if, along with the other members of the Glove Department, I had been able to undertake a planned charabanc visit there in 1958. Unfortunately, just two days before we were due to leave, influenza broke out in Sporting Goods and we had to cancel the trip in order to cover for them. Still, my impression, from the brochures we were given all that time ago, was of a city of elegant shops, street cafes and statues of little boys relieving themselves, not one of burly individuals in Shetland jumpers hung about with rucksacks and climbing-ropes. Despite our not being able to find it in the atlas, Roger is adamant that the Butter Mountain exists, and what is more he is determined to conquer it. He was very offhand with Letitia Odette, who popped in so that we could check her passport was up to date, when she said that this mountain was actually made of butter. I must confess I too thought this a ridiculous suggestion. Who, I asked her, in their right minds would want to create a mountain of butter? Butter Mountain would just be its name, like Table Mountain or Sugar Loaf Mountain; after all, nobody expects these to be made out of table tops or sugar loaves. I could see that Letitia was far from convinced, and in order to settle the matter she asked that I drop a line to Mr Jonathan Aitken M.P. who she saw on television recently and thinks was introduced as the Chairman of the European Support Group (although more trouble with her hearing aid made the catching of his exact title difficult). Dutifully I write to Mr Aitken, at the same time passing on Roger's inquiries as to the Butter Mountain's exact location in Brussels and (in a more technical vein) whether the ascent is a 'boots' or 'cleats' face.

Friday, 22 June

A letter arrives from the Milk Marketing Board. Apparently they do not wish to handle 'Le Fromage européen'. This is bad news, as without a great deal of promotion the product will have to sell on its merits alone, and quite frankly, while we may persuade people to try it once, I cannot see them being in a hurry to do so a second time. One good result of Mr Oliver's bout of 'Odette Belly', as Mr Bridger describes the effects of this cheese on the digestive system, is that it has subdued our lodger, who yesterday even offered to help pack Ingrid's plaster Boadiceas, which we are taking along with some other items – blackcurrant jam, courgettes, and the inevitable cos lettuce – to Fontainebleau as samples of our wares. Roger commented sourly that Mr Oliver's change in behaviour was almost certainly due to his being short of the energy necessary to cause mischief. In the circumstances I shall withhold the information that yesterday, while looking for some paper to wrap Ingrid's models, our paying guest used the first set of completed stamp designs that Roger had unwisely left on the dining-room table. Any inquest on this matter will just have to wait until our return from foreign parts when, hopefully having conquered the Butter Mountain, Roger will be in a better humour.

The second post brings more bad news from Sir Richard Cave at Rolls-Royce. They do not have anything suitable for our requirements. I had almost decided that, protocol or no protocol, the heads of government would just have to walk to the house, when Roger reminded me that during Pope John Paul the Second's visit to Canterbury, some years ago, he travelled through the city in a specially built glass-sided vehicle. While I remember well some of the aspects of His Holiness's visit – the papal helicopter flying low over our garden to land on the recreation ground amid the hot-dog and soft-drink stalls and before a crowd who had been regally (or should it be pontifically?) entertained by Mr Bert Weedon, an ageing guitarist, and some apparently popular singers called the Brotherhood of Man – we did not actually catch sight of the Pope. Indeed it was only after we had strategically stationed ourselves outside Wilf's Tropical Fish Shop in the aptly named St Peter's Street, and waited two hours, cameras at the ready, that we learned that a gas leak had caused the

MILK MARKETING BOARD
TEL. 01·398 4101
TELEX 928239

**THAMES DITTON
SURREY
KT7 OEL**

15 June 1984

Mr W. Morgan Petty
3 Cherry Drive
Canterbury
Kent

Dear Mr Morgan Petty

The Chairman has asked me to acknowledge your
letter dated 8 June.

He suggests you may wish to contact an
advertising agency to handle your marketing
problem.

Yours sincerely

Secretary to
Sir Stephen Roberts
Chairman

SIR RICHARD CAVE
CHAIRMAN

VICKERS P.L.C.
VICKERS HOUSE,
MILLBANK TOWER,
LONDON, SWIP 4RA
TELEPHONE: OI-828 7777

15th June 1984

W. Morgan Petty Esq.,
3, Cherry Drive,
CANTERBURY,
Kent.

Dear Mr. Morgan Petty,

      Thank you for your letter of
10th June. I regret Rolls-Royce Motors
are quite unable to help you as we have
nothing at all suitable for the requirement
you say you have.

      Yours sincerely,

re-routeing of the returning procession. Roger says that as far as he knows the vehicle used by the Pontiff on this occasion and dubbed by the popular press the 'Popemobile' was manufactured by British Leyland. I have therefore dropped a line to the Chairman of that company, Sir Austin Bide, to see whether, in the circumstances, they could help us by producing something similar for our talks. Roger, following I am afraid the example of the tabloid newspapers, suggests that we might christen this the 'Lupinmobile'. Furthermore, Roger also tells me that because of some peculiarity in the pricing system it is actually cheaper to buy motor cars, including those manufactured in this country, abroad. I have therefore also dropped a line to Mr Anthony Fraser, at the Society of Motor Manufacturers and Traders, to see whether there are any financial advantages in taking delivery of our Lupinmobile on the Continent and re-importing it ourselves.

Saturday, 23 June

A very early start on our long journey to La Belle France. Leaving Roger to lash the last of the luggage to the roof-rack I check that all our travellers are present and correct. Viola's legs being what they are, Letitia's will represent them both, and I am very pleased to learn that she has packed a hamper. Mr Bridger, still unhappy that he agreed to accompany us when not entirely sober, mutters quietly in the corner. I notice that he has suddenly grown a great deal around the waist, and on inquiry find this due to his wearing a locking money-belt. My suggestion that such a precaution is not necessary is met with an icy stare and the warning that 'you can't be too careful amongst foreigners'. I did ask Roger, whose idea it was that Mr Bridger should make the trip, if it would not be better for all concerned if he stayed behind. I am not persuaded by his argument that travel will broaden Mr Bridger's mind, or by his further assertion that if the Butter Mountain proves exceptionally difficult Mr Bridger will make an excellent Sherpa.

Ingrid is late and arrives carrying a large bundle of leaflets. They are copies of her very latest epic poem, 'Women rise up and assert yourselves by becoming locomotive drivers' (one hundred and ten verses), translated into French. My plea that what with the five of us and the luggage, not to mention our samples and Roger's climbing gear, there is really not enough room for this literature in the Morris Minor brings forth a tirade that we are 'conspiring in the international subjugation of women'. In the end Ingrid, seeing my resolution, plays her final card and bursts into tears. Anxious that we should not miss our ferry I agree to take the leaflets and leave behind instead the two deck-chairs. All I can hope is that Monsieur Mitterrand has enough seats of his own. Just as we are finally ready to pull away the postman arrives with the mail, which I read on the way to Dover. I am grateful to find that my best wishes have served Mrs Barbara Castle well and that she has been re-elected to the European Parliament. I shall make a point of getting a seat near her in that institution as she seems a very kindly and helpful lady and I am sure would be just the sort of person to show me the ropes.

By mid afternoon we have arrived in Calais (1347 captured by Edward III of England). Unfortunately, not aware that duty-free alcohol is allowed off the ship, Mr Bridger had taken advantage of the reduced prices and rather overdone things in the bar – a fact which became obvious when, in response to the French customs officer's perfectly civil question about whether he had anything to declare, he replied loudly that indeed he had. I shall not dwell on the exact nature of the riposte except to say that it was uncomplimentary to the French nation in general and to the official in particular. Two hours later, ourselves and the vehicle having been thoroughly searched, we are allowed to leave the port, minus I might add the box of cos lettuce, for which it seems we did not have the necessary agricultural documentation – an annoying piece of petty bureaucracy which has deprived Europe's leaders of their first taste of our produce and is something I shall raise at Fontainebleau. It was my intention to give Mr Bridger, the author of this incident, a piece of my mind, but no sooner are we on our way than he falls into a deep sleep, punctuated, much to everyone's annoyance and despite a number of sharp jabs in the ribs, by loud rasping snores.

Once out on the open road we are hampered by the fact that our atlas, while containing a great deal of valuable information, does stop at the Battle of Waterloo in 1815, and any roads built subsequently are not shown. Roger, eager to experience driving on the 'wrong side of the road', takes the wheel. After some twenty minutes of not getting very far, and having passed the same roundabout five times, I venture to suggest that we may be travelling in the wrong direction. Roger, narrowly missing an articulated lorry loaded with live chickens, blames any error on the road signs which, he says, as everybody knows, were turned around by the population during the war to confuse the Germans and can't have all been put back properly. I think this is a poor excuse and suggest that we stop and ask somebody for directions. Reaching back to the days of his O-level French, he carefully prepares the question and stops at the next person we meet. As luck would have it his preparation was unnecessary as we find ourselves addressing a coach driver from Inverness holidaying in the area. Our further good fortune is that, while our new friend now spends his time transporting passengers around the Highlands, his former occupation was to ferry hordes of sun-seeking holidaymakers to Marseilles and all points east. In no time he has given Roger full directions to our destination, and we offer our thanks and a pot of blackcurrant jam. He looked a little blank however when Letitia, still mindful of Roger's earlier remark, congratulated him on driving so extensively in a country whose road signs had not recovered from the German occupation.

Sunday, 24 June

3 a.m. finds us motoring gently down the Route Nationale Une towards Paris. Our trip up until this time had been

Member
of the European Parliament

From The Rt Hon Mrs Barbara Castle MEP

18 June 1984

Mr W Morgan Petty
3 Cherry Drive
Canterbury
Kent

Dear Morgan Petty

Your good luck message reached me this morning on my return from
the count in Greater Man chester West last night.

It was kind of you to send me your good wishes. I hope you are
as pleased with the result as I am.

Yours sincerely

Barbara Castle

without incident, except for a brief stop at a garage for some petrol, where Mr Bridger, now awake, discovered, much to his embarrassment, that he had left the key to his lockable money-belt at home on the kitchen table. However, having passed through the town of Amiens (431 headquarters of Clodian the Hairy) we suffer a puncture. Now it is time for my confession. In order to accommodate first the deck-chairs, and latterly Ingrid's poems, I had also left something behind: the spare tyre. It is light before our urgent waving-down of vehicles results in assistance from a local farmer. In order that we may jack up the Morris and remove the wheel for repair, it is necessary for us to unload it. Our French friend, François, offers, most kindly, to take the 'pneu' back to Amiens. Mr Bridger is against this, stating quite forcibly that if we let what he calls 'this shifty-looking frog' take our tyre away we may never see it again. I am left in something of a quandary. If we do let the wheel go we may, as Mr Bridger predicts, be left stranded, but if we do not, we shall be equally marooned. Fortunately Roger resolves the dilemma by suggesting that he and I accompany François and the tyre back into town.

Upon our return I am pleasantly surprised to find Letitia and Ingrid doing a brisk roadside trade with passing motorists. In the ninety minutes of our absence they have sold twelve jars of jam, three pounds of courgettes, and seven pasties. I am even more confident now of the success our produce will enjoy just as soon as we set out our stall at the Common Market. Not seeing any models of Queen Boadicea on the display, I ask Ingrid whether she has been successful in selling out. The answer is no, and what is more, she tells me angrily, she will not be able to sell any of her models of the Queen of the Iceni on this trip as someone has painted beards and moustaches on them, quite incongruous with their other obviously female features. I am thankful that she does not consider any of the present company the culprit, although I would not like to be in Mr Oliver's shoes when we return.

At last Fontainebleau (1814 site of Napoleon Bonaparte's abdication). I must say Mr Bridger's attitude to France seems to have mellowed. Maybe Roger was right and travelling has broadened his mind, or it could just be the discovery that in this country a very drinkable wine can be had for fifty pence a bottle. Any suggestion that one litre before breakfast and another two before lunch may be overdoing things is greeted with the reply that wine-tasting is his hobby and, as we have so little time, getting an early start is imperative. Unfortunately he has not yet been able to find a way of unlocking his money-belt, and his 'hobby' is proving rather expensive for the rest of us. Although he has promised to pay it all back when we get home, Roger is concerned that he will forget, not an altogether unlikely prospect as he seems to have no recollection of the thirty francs he borrowed from me yesterday. Indeed I would go so far as to say that his recollection of doing anything yesterday is doubtful. Letitia on the other hand says that we should encourage Mr Bridger in this pursuit, as she understands that there are millions of gallons of surplus wine in Europe which is giving the Common Market Commissioners a very big headache. If they are seeking to reduce the amount by drinking it half as fast as Mr Bridger is, then I am not surprised they are feeling unwell. Fortunately, during his last bout of over-indulgence he misplaced his corkscrew, and it may well be that this will slow him down.

After two nights spent camping I decide that we should tidy up before presenting ourselves at the château. We find a small cafe and, having completed our ablutions, enjoy a lunch of something called *escargots* (which look a bit like snails) and *lapin*. Roger does not get as far as the *lapin*, for no sooner has he eaten the bread put down beside him for the *escargots* than the waiter brings some more. Mindful that we are guests in the country, and not wishing to seem ungrateful, Roger consumes three long loaves before finally giving up.

At two o'clock we set off for the historic encounter. I

confess to being a little nervous at meeting all these heads of government, but as Letitia points out they probably feel the same way about meeting me. We have gone barely fifty yards before we are stopped by two members of the local constabulary, one tall with a thick moustache, the other small and wiry and wearing a black leather trench coat. Unfortunately their command of English is not great, and it is left to Roger to translate as best he can in rusty French. The gendarmerie seem somewhat startled to learn that we are the official delegation from 3 Cherry Drive and that I am a duly elected member of the European Parliament. Roger is just going on to explain about the mix-up with my invitation to the talks and the *Reader's Digest* book offers when two other policemen appear. A hurried conversation takes place, after which we are instructed to hand over the boxes we are carrying. As I continue to protest at the delay (I do not want to be late for my first Euro-summit) the policemen prise open the pasties and examine each of the courgettes in turn. Quite what they had hoped to find eludes me, but the result is that the pasties are ruined and some of the specially made presentation labels on the jam are torn.

Angered by this most unfriendly of welcomes I approach the trench-coated policeman, who seems to be the one in charge, and give him a piece of my mind, and furthermore suggest that if he would just telephone Mrs Thatcher or Monsieur Mitterrand, the whole matter could be cleared up instantly. A further huddled conference between themselves and we are instructed, according to Roger's translation, to 'push off'. I was trying very hard to keep things calm when Mr Bridger, having doubled his lunchtime consumption of red wine, became extremely agitated and intervened vigorously shouting at the diminutive custodian of Gallic law and order that 'there were no closed doors on D-Day'. I have to admit that I found Mr Bridger's first-hand knowledge of the Normandy landings somewhat surprising as I had always understood from Mrs Bridger, before her flight to Bolton, that her husband had spent the sixth of June 1944 making plum duff in Catterick. Whatever the merits of Mr Bridger's war record, this outburst was sufficient to have us somewhat unceremoniously escorted away from the gates of the château and ordered to leave the area immediately or face the consequences. Mr Bridger, his blood now up, and armed with a box of courgettes, was keen on the latter course but I thought it prudent for us to make a quick, strategic, withdrawal.

There is little more to say about this our first, unhappy venture into Europe. I did try telephoning the château myself but without success. I had rather hoped that the prospect of Roger's ascent of the Butter Mountain would lift our little group's flagging spirits, but any prospect of this evaporated when a loud knocking noise developed in the engine just outside Rouen (1481 Martyrdom of St Joan) and we were left to limp slowly towards the Channel port and home. The only person who seems to have derived direct benefit from the trip was Ingrid, who, during one of our innumerable stops to ask directions, met a young Frenchwoman called Ghislaine who belonged to an organization very grandly entitled 'La Société pour l'extinction de l'homme'. So well did they get on during the half-hour it took us to find we had been going hopelessly the wrong way that Ingrid even gave her new friend a model of Boadicea, beard and all. La Société pour l'extinction de l'homme? I must remember to ask Roger what it means.

Wednesday, 27 June

As Mr Frank Sinatra so elegantly puts it in the song, 'It's very nice to go travelling but so much nicer to come home.' My first act today is to pen a very strongly worded note of protest to the French President. While I accept that security at these Euro-gatherings is vitally important, it does somewhat seem to defeat the object of the exercise if it is so tight that bona fide representatives of Common Market members, like ourselves, cannot get through to attend the discussions. Furthermore I take Monsieur Mitterrand to task over the pasties and home-made jam. Although she did not say anything I could see that Letitia was most upset at the fate of these after all the hard work she and her sister had put into them. I suppose it is too much to expect that my absence went unnoticed by the other heads of government, and what I now fear is that they, in turn, may stay away from our little gathering in a fit of pique. To try and avoid this, at least in his case, I end my letter to the French President on a conciliatory note by apologizing for Mr Bridger's behaviour, both at Fontainebleau and at a restaurant on the way home, where, convinced that he had been short-changed, he banged his hand on the counter with such force that a picture fell from the wall and shattered a fish tank.

Fortunately the great arguments that I feared would take place between Ingrid and Roger and Mr Oliver have been averted by our 'paying guest's' decision to leave. When we return home there is a note to this effect on the kitchen table. Apparently he has gone to take up what he describes as 'an exciting opportunity in tinned fruit'. The note goes on to say he knows how much we shall miss him. Surveying the kitchen sink, piled high in our absence with dirty crockery, and examining the electric toaster, which seems to be full of golden syrup, I very much doubt it.

Friday, 29 June

This morning's post brings two letters. The first is from Mr Francis Pym who, due to pressure of work, will, disappointingly, be unable to act as our adviser at the Lupin Talks. The second is from Basil de Ferranti, Member of the European Parliament and Vice President of its Kangaroo Group. I am sorry to learn from Mr de Ferranti that his group is not, as Letitia Odette had suggested, concerned with increasing the marsupial population of the European Community but with abolishing trade barriers. While I am sure this is a very laudable aim, their function will come as a bitter disappointment to Roger, who I think had rather seen a kangaroo as the substitute for the goat I refused to let him have. It is not that

From: The Rt. Hon. Francis Pym, M.C., M.P.

House of Commons,
London, SW1A OAA

19th June, 1984.

Dear Mr. Morgan Petty,

Mr. Pym has asked me to thank
you very much for your letter. He
appreciates what you say, but much
regrets that he will not be able
to act as your adviser at the
forthcoming 'lupin talks'. He is
sorry, but I am sure you will
appreciate that he is exceptionally
busy at the present time.

Yours sincerely,

Private Secretary.

W. Morgan Petty,
 3 Cherry Drive,
Canterbury,
KENT.

European Parliament

Basil de Ferranti MEP
Millbank Tower
London SW1P 4QS

Telephone 01: 834 6611
Telex: 264055

20 June 1984

W Morgan Petty Esq
3 Cherry Drive
CANTERBURY
Kent

Dear Mr Petty

Many thanks for your most entertaining letter.

I enclose a copy of the Kangaroo Group's brochure. As you say,
our objectives are somewhat different to the ones that you
thought that we were on about!

Yours sincerely

Basil de Ferranti

I have anything against goats but I did fear that, should it escape, it could wreak havoc in the garden. I also had another reason which I kept to myself. Having recently read that Mr Michael Jopling, the Secretary of State for Agriculture, had announced plans to spend some fifty million pounds paying farmers to keep less cattle, and in that way reduce the Common Market milk surplus, I wrote to Mr Jopling making what I consider to have been the very sound suggestion that he extend these payments to people like us here at 3 Cherry Drive who did not keep livestock at all and were blameless even for the current surplus. As yet I have not received a reply. It may well be that this has gone astray in the post, but certainly I would not wish to jeopardize any chance of a cheque, however small, by being found in possession of a milk-producing nanny.

Monday, 2 July

With only a little light weeding to do in the garden, and while the weather remains fine, Roger and myself spend the afternoon laying out the position of the Euro-tower. As luck has it we have just enough bricks left over from the greenhouse extension to outline the base. Standing back, it is not difficult to imagine the magnificent concrete and glass structure, with revolving vegetarian restaurant, that will one day occupy this site. Now that we have moved the compost heap we are left with a space adjacent to the azaleas of some forty feet by ten. My first thought, given the popularity of the Odette sisters' blackcurrant jam, is that we might plant this area with some bushes to provide them with the necessary fruit. I take the opportunity this afternoon of dropping in to discuss the matter.

By the most fortunate of coincidences Letitia, stimulated by our recent membership and aided by the *Financial Times*, has been closely studying investment patterns in Common Market countries. She tells me that, while she is grateful for my offer, I might do much better to forgo any further thoughts of blackcurrants, redesignate the reclaimed area as an industrial zone, and seek to attract overseas investment. According to Letitia, if we were to undertake such a course, then 3 Cherry Drive would become eligible for all manner of industrial and commercial grants, enabling us to build a manufacturing plant on our spare piece of ground. I must confess that I am somewhat sceptical about all this; furthermore, what would we do with a factory? There are of course Roger's plaster models but, however unkind it may sound, my view of this is that further production space would simply result in failure on a larger scale, and we already have six boxes of less than perfect specimens of his work hidden away in the attic. I have obviously missed the point, for Letitia explains that it would not be us that would occupy the factory but a multinational company. Fearing there is no other way to make sense of this than to show my own ignorance, why, I ask, should a multinational company wish to start production of its goods at the end of my garden? The answer, it seems, is tariff barriers. If such a multinational were to begin manufacture alongside the azaleas, the resulting output could be sold within the Common Market without incurring any such penalties.

I tried to look as if I was following Letitia's argument, but the truth is that I had become hopelessly lost very soon after her opening sentence. It is all very confusing, but I have learned in the last few months that nothing concerning the Common Market is anything but that. Certainly Letitia's explanation sounded plausible, and the revenue that she claims we will receive in rent and rates from the establishment of such a complex would come in very handy. Sensing, I think, that I was not entirely happy with her proposals she suggested that I discuss the matter with Roger and then, if we decided to go ahead, she would assist us in any way she could.

I gave some thought to this matter on the way home. One of my main concerns is having the garden full of large numbers of boiler-suited factory workers eating their sandwiches and playing impromptu games of football, with heaven knows what damage to the flower beds, a reservation that I voice to Roger when I raise the matter. Surprisingly, he is able to put my mind at rest on this score. Manufacturing plants these days, especially of a size no greater than forty foot by ten, he says, do not have workers as such. Thanks to microchip technology the whole process can be carried out by a computerized robot, no bigger than a hatbox. Any manual activity is restricted to routine maintenance – oiling the tappets, changing the plugs, etc. – and as he expresses his willingness to undertake such activities, it would seem that we could have our factory without a single outsider needing to set foot on our property. The only question that remains now is who to ask? After some discussion the prime candidates for this sort of investment would seem to be the Japanese and the Americans. I shall ask Letitia for her help in soliciting investment both from the land of the Rising Sun (Nissan and Toyota) and from the United States of America (General Motors and Ford), where we can offer the latter the chance to become Ford of America, Great Britain and Cherry Drive.

Wednesday, 4 July

The knocking sound under the Morris Minor's bonnet, which first began on our ill-fated trip to France, grows daily louder, until even on short journeys we are accompanied by a constant syncopation. The reason for this has, despite several exhaustive examinations of the vehicle, left Roger foxed. Unable to stand the noise or the startled looks from pedestrians any longer, he has taken our car to the garage. It is a somewhat shamefaced part-time gardener who returns to explain that far from being the 'big end' or 'worn heads' or any of his other dire predictions, the trouble had been caused by a foreign object in the engine. Indeed it turns out that the object is not so foreign as all that, being Mr Bridger's errant corkscrew which has become wedged behind the battery. Roger asks if we should return the corkscrew? I have to admit that relations between ourselves and Mr Bridger are still strained after Fontainebleau, a situation not helped by his failure, deliberate or otherwise, to reimburse us for the money he borrowed then.

Head of UK Offices: 24 May 1984   *Telephone: 01-222 8122*
George Scott   *Telex: 23208 EURUK.G.*

Mr. W. Morgan Petty,
3 Cherry Drive,
Canterbury,
Kent.

Dear Mr. Morgan Petty,

        Thank you very much for writing to me as suggested by
Vice-President Christopher Tugendhat. Much as I would like to be
able to help you, my strong feeling is that this is just the kind of
issue where the European Parliament could exercise beneficent influence,
and it so happens that my opposite number, who is the head of the
European Parliament office in London and is also called Roger - Mr.
Roger Broad - is particularly interested in the question of fruit
trees and the grafting thereof. Without wishing to pass you on like
some unwanted parcel, may I recommend that you should make contact
with him at his London office, 2 Queen Anne's Gate, London SW1.

                        Yours sincerely,

                        George Scott

Cardiff Office: *Belfast Office:*   *Edinburgh Office:*
4 Cathedral Road   Windsor House   7 Alva Street
Cardiff CF1 9SG   9/15 Bedford Street   Edinburgh EH2 4PH
Telephone: 0222-371631   Belfast N. Ireland   Telephone: 031-225 2058
                                 Telephone: 0232-240708

However I am aware that he has few equals with the secateurs and pruning saw, and the cordon of Cox's apples badly needs attention. I therefore suggest that I will offer Mr Bridger the corkscrew back on condition that he settle the garage bill, some twelve pounds sixty pence plus V.A.T., and that we will have to regard the loans made in France as the price to be paid for a continued good crop of eating apples.

The post brings a reply from the Director of the Royal Military School of Music. My original plan was to greet the heads of government when they arrived by helicopter with an honour guard of Roger, his nearly new garden fork raised in salute, while Viola Odette played martial tunes on the cottage upright. However, given Viola's condition, and naturally wishing to make the very best of first impressions, I sought help from the R.M.S.M., who I thought might lend me a band (being students, I also secretly hoped that, grateful for the opportunity to play on such an auspicious occasion, they would do so on an expenses-only basis). Unfortunately Lieutenant Colonel Beat (what a very appropriate name) explains that they endeavour to keep their outside commitments to a minimum. Such a reply may present me with a problem. Carried away by images of the Changing of the Guard and Trooping the Colour and thinking that Roger might look faintly ridiculous standing there alone on parade while several hundred military bandsmen played 'Imperial Echoes', I also wrote to the Regimental Adjutant of the Coldstream Guards with a request to borrow some soldiers. I calculated that we might need about two dozen, just enough for the heads of government to walk up and down a row. Now, without a military band, we are left to face the prospect, if the Coldstream Guards do decide to come, of having a series of Prime Ministers escorted through massed ranks of these ramrod-straight figures in their brightly coloured tunics, with arms sloped, while Viola (legs willing) pounds out 'Soldiers of the Queen' on the piano.

I am pondering on this when Ingrid calls in with the news that her friend Jaz has been acquitted on the charge of assault.

ROYAL MILITARY SCHOOL OF MUSIC

Kneller Hall Twickenham Middlesex TW2 7DU

Telephone 01-898 5533/4

W Morgan Petty Esq
3 Cherry Drive
Canterbury
KENT

Your reference

Our reference   DM/4501/5

Date **29** June 1984

Dear Mr Morgan Petty,

Thank you for your letter of 14th June.

I regret that Kneller Hall is unable to assist you
by providing a band. We are a training establishment
and endeavour to keep outside commitments to an absolute
minimum in order not to disrupt our programme of
studies.

With best wishes,

Yours sincerely,

D R BEAT
Lieutenant Colonel
Director of Music

Apparently the jury found it impossible to believe that a female of just under five foot could have manhandled two burly policemen in the way alleged. According to Ingrid it took the 'twelve good persons and true' just five minutes to reach their verdict, and the whole thing would have been over in hours had it not taken most of the morning for Jaz to read out the oath.

Friday, 6 July

Along with the benefits of membership of the Common Market go, inevitably, responsibilities. I learn from a programme on Channel Four (novel in my experience in that I understand every word spoken) that as members of this market we are governed by the provisions of something called the Lomé Conventions. It seems that the first of these conventions allows for the importation into Common Market territory of agricultural goods from developing countries on a duty-free basis. I must say that I think this is a splendid idea, and certainly we here at 3 Cherry Drive have no objection to being party to such an agreement. However, the second convention extends this cooperation to include sea transport, mineral production and investment protection. Having no sea transport or minerals, and with our investment limited to a few pounds in the Post Office, I hardly feel that we are in a position to assist anybody in these areas. Still, I am sure that it is the principle that counts, and so I write to the Directorate-General for Development, in Brussels, to see if there are provisions for people in our position who fall between the first and second convention, a sort of Lomé one and a half.

This evening I draw up a list of developing countries – Australia, New Zealand, Zimbabwe (formerly named after Cecil Rhodes: I wonder if Mr Zimbabwe too was an explorer?) – making it plain that we are willing to accept, within the limits of our culinary usage and without duplication of vegetables that we ourselves have in surplus, whatever agricultural products they may wish to send. Hopefully we can look forward in the near future to receiving from Mr Bob Hawke, the Australian Premier, a quantity of passion fruit and especially walnuts as Roger, who is very good in the kitchen, has an excellent recipe for Melbourne pancakes in which he uses quite a lot of these. Furthermore, I am anxious to know whether in the case of New Zealand the term 'agricultural products' extends to sheep's fleeces. During the dark evenings of last winter Letitia Odette rediscovered the art of spinning, making Roger a very nice pullover from the wool of a Kent Brown. I have therefore asked Mr Muldoon, the Prime Minister of that country, if they could let us have some of these. If he agrees to help I have no doubt that the industrious Letitia will soon have us kitted out as walking advertisements for the wool trade down under.

On the question of things antipodean, another missive arrives from the Kangaroo Group. They ask if they may be allowed to publish my letter in the next edition of their newspaper. Naturally I agree; it is good to see we are being taken seriously at last.

Sunday, 8 July

I return home from a very unsatisfactory encounter with Mr Bridger. He refuses to settle the garage bill and when I, in turn, threaten to withhold the corkscrew he says that I am most welcome to keep it as he has already bought a replacement. No sooner have I opened the front door than I am engulfed in a cacophony of loud guitar music. I find Roger in the living room with Justin. Shouting to overcome the noise from the wireless, he explains that Justin is a friend of Pauline, Viola Odette's home chiropodist, and that he has come to discuss our Euro-tower. Discussion of anything is impossible with the wireless volume full up, and despite Justin's pleas that 'hearing the sounds helps him to get his head around things', I prevail upon Roger to turn it down. Justin tells me that he is 'plugged into radio in a big way', by which I assume he means it is his consuming interest, and that he wants to

Basil de Ferranti MEP
Ferranti plc
Millbank Tower
LONDON SW1P 4QS

Kangaroo Group ~

(THE MOVEMENT FOR FREE MOVEMENT)

3 July 1984

W Morgan Petty Esq
3 Cherry Drive
CANTERBURY
Kent

Dear Mr Petty

Mr de Ferranti passed me a copy of your letter of 22 May. I do
wish that all the letters we received gave us half as much
enjoyment as yours. You will indeed be a breath of fresh air if
you continue to carry on your dealings with the Common Market in
the way you have started off.

The fundamental objective of the Kangaroo Group is to ensure that
just as you would be entitled to take up a vacant pitch in the
market in Maidstone, so should you be able to take one in Calais
or Ostende.

When we decided to call ourselves the Kangaroo Group we were
thinking of that animal's ability to leap over barriers and give
them a good, hard kick with their hind legs in the process: we
forgot that that animal also has legs suitable for pulling.

Please tactfully tell Letitia that she did indeed get the wrong
end of the stick, but please reassure her that we are trying to
ensure that when she tries to sell her jam and pasties across the
Channel, she will not run into any barriers with the various
national hygiene laws.

Vice-Presidents:
Basil de Ferranti, European Parliament Office, 2 Queen Anne's Gate, London SW1H 9AA, England.
Kai Nyborg, Europa-Parlamentets Informationskontorer, Børsen DK-1217, Kobenhavn K, Danmark.
Dieter Rogalla, Informationsburos des Europaischen Parlaments, In der Raste 12, 5300 Bonn 1, Deutschland.
Karl von Wogau, Informationsburos des Europaischen Parlaments, In der Raste 12, 5300 Bonn 1, Deutschland.

I enclose a copy of the latest issue of "Kangaroo News", and have
put you on the mailing list for future editions.

So that we may give our other 30,000 readers as much fun as we
have had, please may we publish your letter in our next edition.

With best wishes to Letitia, her sisters, Roger and Mr Bridger.
Please keep writing.

Yours sincerely

Pamela Entwistle
Kangaroo Group

Enc

'put out a few watts of his own'. After an hour of careful translation I am reasonably sure that what Justin would like is to open a radio station using our tower to broadcast the signal. It is certainly a novel idea but, as I explain, one that will require a great deal of thought. After all, I know nothing about radio stations. According to Justin my answer is 'cool', but he says that I should not worry too much over the day-to-day running of the station as he has plenty of experience in that direction. To illustrate this fact he draws my attention to the logo on his T-shirt. I have to admit that, during the course of our conversation, I had become somewhat intrigued by this design, a whale with a radio aerial protruding from its blowhole, but hesitated to ask its significance. It is, so Justin informs me proudly, the official T-shirt of Radio Leviathan, a ship-based radio station for which he had worked as something called the senior disc jockey. I must say I am quite impressed by this. Furthermore, as Justin points out, having a radio station at the bottom of the garden has all sorts of advantages, not the least of which is instant access to millions all over Europe whom we could keep informed of the progress here at 3 Cherry Drive. I promise that if he comes back next week, I will let him have my answer. As I leave, to deal with some urgent European correspondence, the house is again filled with loud electronic music. I seem to remember reading somewhere that music was capable of soothing the savage brow; equally, I reflect, it can give you a headache.

Monday, 9 July

Today we hold a full-scale dress rehearsal for welcoming the European heads of government to 3 Cherry Drive, Canterbury, for the Lupin Talks. It hardly seems worth dragging the piano out into the garden, especially as the forecast is for drizzle. We therefore place Viola on a stool, from where she promises to la la loudly in the appropriate places. Not knowing yet whether we will be blessed with the presence of the Coldstream Guards, I tell Roger to imagine himself as about twenty-five men. Shortage of personnel also makes the next bit a little tricky. I have to play not only myself as the welcoming host but the sundry heads of government being welcomed. All in all I do not think it bad for a first rehearsal, and Roger's idea of fixing the hair-dryer to the Bramley apple so that, when turned on, it simulated the draught from the rotor blades of a helicopter, was a very nice touch.

As all good rehearsals should, ours shows up the areas in which we could improve. The first is Viola's music. While I agree that 'Here we are again, happy as can be' is very popular, given the discordant note so very often struck at European summits is she sure, I ask, that it is entirely appropriate? The second problem arises on the always difficult subject of protocol. From my observation of such things on television it seems you hug the Italians, shake hands with the Germans and kiss the French on both cheeks. Quite what you do with the Greeks I am not sure, and a complete mystery surrounds the official form of welcome for the Danes. Then there is the question of female visitors: are they to be kissed on the cheek or on the hand, à la Charles Boyer? Roger compounds my concern with his suggestion that there may well be some time-honoured and secret form of physical address between senior politicians, like there is in freemasonry. Certainly I would not wish to make a mistake at the very outset of the talks and jeopardize our chance of a lupin subsidy. Fearing that just such a problem would arise, I wrote recently to His Royal Highness Prince Charles for guidance. If anyone can give us a few pointers in this area I am sure His Royal Highness can, for as Roger says he has probably hugged and kissed more heads of state than we have had hot dinners. I await his response with some disquiet; protocol or no protocol, neither Roger nor myself views with any great enthusiasm the thought of kissing Mrs Thatcher anywhere. I have also extended invitations to attend, with observer status only, to Mr Neil Kinnock, the Labour leader, and Mr Caspar Weinberger, the U.S. Secretary of Defence. I can only hope they reply very soon, as allocating bed-space is proving very difficult despite

Roger's introduction of a graph covered with coloured pins and sticky tape.

Thursday, 12 July

The post brings two letters. The first is from Jonathan Aitken M.P. He explains that he is, far from being Chairman of the European Support Group, Chairman of the European Reform Group. We really must do something about Letitia's hearing aid. He tells me that this reform group seeks to do away with butter mountains, wine lakes and rape forests. I am not altogether sure how that will go down with the climbers, swimmers and nature ramblers within the Community. The second letter is from the Ministry of Culture in France. Being in French, it will have to await Roger's return for translation. It is a good job that things are slack in the garden, as this is the third afternoon this week that he has been out. He claims to be spending this time in the city library studying European history, but I suspect that any studying he is doing is in the company of Justin and on the subject of popular music. Further evidence for this is abandonment of his stripy Continental-style jumper in favour of a T-shirt with what he tells me is a portrait of 'Dylan' on it, although what wearing a very poor likeness of a Welsh poet has to do with popular music I am not entirely sure.

I have to confess surprise that we have not yet received replies from the United States or Japan concerning our industrial zone. From the way Letitia Odette spoke I had imagined hordes of senior executives from the multinational companies beating a path to my door, but up until now we have not had a single inquiry. It could well be the post, but there is another strong possibility that the industry which would have come here to 3 Cherry Drive is being lured to other areas by means of larger subsidies and fringe benefits. Viola Odette did offer to help by providing free lunches for the workforce (even, in the case of the Japanese, bowls of raw fish) but, as I pointed out to her, there was not going to be a

From: JONATHAN AITKEN, M.P.

HOUSE OF COMMONS
LONDON SWIA OAA

Ref : JWPA/ay

4th July 1984

W. Morgan Petty Esq.
3 Cherry Drive
Canterbury
Kent

Dear Mr. Petty

Thank you for your most amusing letter of 19th June. I
wish you well in all your diplomatic and mountaineering
negotiations with the Common Market, although like you I
do not have much faith in the whole concept.

Far from being "Chairman of something called 'The European
Support Group'", I am in fact Chairman of the Conservative
European Reform Group which among other things seeks to
do away with butter mountains, wine lakes, rape forrests etc.

Unfortunately, there are strict rules of Parliamentary
protocol which make it impossible for me to follow up your
letter with any direct action as you are not a constituent
of mine, but of Mr. David Crouch MP, the MP for Canterbury.
I have forwarded your letter to him. I am sure he will be
glad to know that one of his constituents has such a
communitaire sense of humour!

With all good wishes.

Yours sincerely

Jonathan Aitken

Jonathan Aitken

Ministère de la Culture

Direction
des Musées de France
—

Palais du Louvre
75041 PARIS CEDEX 01
Tél. : 260.39.26

DMF/BCD/ ___923___ /MR/NH/

- 5 JUIL. 1984

Monsieur,

        Vous avez bien voulu par lettre du 11 avril 1984,
me faire part de votre projet d'exposition de peintures
du dix-neuvième siècle.

        J'ai le regret de vous faire savoir qu'il m'est
impossible de répondre favorablement à votre demande. En
effet, les musées français ne prêtent des oeuvres que
dans le cas d'expositions temporaires à caractère culturel,
organisées par des personnes publiques ou des organismes
à vocation culturelle, présentant toutes les garanties de
sécurité nécessaires à la présentation d'oeuvres d'art.

        Veuillez agréer, Monsieur, l'assurance de ma consi-
dération distinguée.

Pour le Directeur des Musées de France
et par délégation
L'Adjoint au Directeur des Musées de France

Dominique CHARVET

Monsieur W. Morgan Petty
3 Cherry Drive
Canterbury (Kent)
0227 Grande-Bretagne

workforce, and so we could hardly expect this to swing things in our favour.

We are left with only one way to enable us to compete, and that is to declare our industrial area a European enterprise zone. Quite what this entails I do not know, but in for a penny, in for a pound. I wrote immediately to Norman Tebbit, the Secretary of State for Trade and Industry, telling him of my decision, and also to Gaston Thorn, President of the European Commission, asking when we might expect to receive a cheque. One thing worries me: if it is as simple as this, why aren't more people with a few square yards of garden doing it? Just to be on the safe side I shall formalize things by having Roger put up a sign alongside the area reading 'Enterprise Zone – Keep Out'.

Saturday, 14 July

A note from the Assistant Private Secretary to His Royal Highness Charles, Prince of Wales, who tells me that His Royal Highness will see my letter at the earliest opportunity. I shall look forward to a prompt reply from our future King as Ingrid has promised to loan me, for the purposes of practising official greetings, the dressmaker's dummy which WAVE have. I must admit that my experience of Ingrid's friends, and a poster that I recently put up in the front window at her request, led me to believe that her women's group meetings were taken up with subjects like 'Female Telepathy' and 'Women and their Position in West African Society', so it is somewhat refreshing to learn that at least some of their time is spent in such homely pursuits as dressmaking. However I made the mistake of congratulating Ingrid on this, only to discover my error. The dressmaking dummy, far from having the obviously practical application, is in fact used to illustrate the enslavement of females in mundane tasks that alienate them from the process of decision-making. One decision that I have made is to keep very quiet in Ingrid's presence in future.

BUCKINGHAM PALACE

From: The Assistant Private Secretary to H.R.H. The Prince of Wales   5th July 1984

Dear Mr Petty

    Thank you for your letter of 30th June to
The Prince of Wales. I have passed it on to His
Royal Highness who will see it at the earliest
opportunity.

Yours sincerely

David Roycroft

David Roycroft

W. Morgan Petty, Esq.

We also receive a letter from Malcolm Rifkind, Minister of State at the Foreign and Commonwealth Office. Roger, who keeps abreast of things in the world of show-business, had informed me that there was an attempt to publicize the existence and activities of the Common Market, and doubtless to boost sales, by a series of theatrical productions. On hearing this, it occurred to me that we might kill two birds with one stone and hold one of these Euro-spectaculars here at the same time as our summit meeting. After a hard day's negotiating I am sure our guests would appreciate such a diversion. If we could arrange something of this nature, it would be a great help, as choosing appropriate after-talks entertainment is proving quite a headache. My original preference was for games of a participatory nature – hunt the thimble and charades. I remember the success these enjoyed when I organized the Men's Wear and Camping and Outdoor Accessories Christmas party in 1962. However Roger was of the opinion that these might prove a little mundane, and in the case of charades he foresaw language difficulties. He suggested instead that we might have a cabaret performed by somebody called Clive James, who he said was 'most amusing'. I must confess that I have never heard of Mr James, although I did once make the acquaintance of a Mr Harry James who was a coach-builder with British Leyland, and I wondered if they might be related. Roger says he thinks this is highly unlikely as Clive James is Australian and introduces a show on Channel Four which starts after almost everyone but night-watchmen and insomniacs have gone to bed. I ask exactly what Mr James's 'being amusing' entailed, and Roger, struggling for an adequate explanation, described this star of late night television as a 'colonial wit', which I suppose means he's a bit like Chips Rafferty.

My letter to Mr Rifkind was to elicit support for the undertaking and to find out what grants might be available for us to employ artistes on such a project. My concern is that, again according to Roger, the only shows that have been staged so far seem to have consisted of mind-reading parrots

OFFICE OF THE UNITED KINGDOM
PERMANENT REPRESENTATIVE
TO THE EUROPEAN COMMUNITIES
ROND-POINT ROBERT SCHUMAN 6
1040 BRUSSELS

TELEPHONE 230 62 05

9 May 1984

Mr W Morgan Petty
3 Cherry Drive
CANTERBURY
Kent

Dear Mr Morgan Pett,

Thank you for your letter of 23 March. I am sorry that, what with
the Easter Holiday and the need to give deep thought to your letter,
it has taken me a little time to reply. In particular, I was uncertain
what significance to attach to your first sentence; and since I am still
no clearer, I shall not attempt to comment on it.

I agree with you about the opportunities available to British people
in the Common Market. We need the entrepreneurial spirit to seize
them. I think there are good prospects in the areas you mention.
The Common Fisheries Policy of the EC provides an excellent framework
for UK fishermen, though I am not sure that it is relevant to your
own situation.

I hope that with "Roger" and Letitia Odette you will be able to prosper
by providing the delights of your local cuisine - oysters and shellfish,
jam and pasties, Kent lamb and fruit and vegetables.

Good wishes,

Yours sincerely,

Michael Butler

Michael Butler

from Westphalia and flea-circuses from the Dordogne. While it is certainly not to my taste, I suppose this sort of event might prove very popular with the heads of government, but I make it clear that however large the subsidy, the whole project is a non-starter if we are forced to employ a Euro-artiste such as Petula Clark or Charles Aznavour or, worst of all, Sacha Distel. Much though it may run against the *esprit communitaire*, I would rather take up Roger's other suggestion, that we use the Lupin Talks as a practice run for the Eurovision Song Contest and subject the assembled heads of government to a rendition of 'The Goldfish Song'.

Sunday, 15 July

I am awakened at five a.m. by a knock on the front door. Bleary-eyed, I discover a very enthusiastic Justin anxious for a decision on the radio station. As I sit in a near-comatose state he reels off facts and figures concerning potential audiences, transmission schedules and demographic income analysis. He has been, in his own rather peculiar jargon, 'getting it together with the cats that jive the computers'. Given my other commitments I have not, as promised, had time to fully consider the implications of having a radio station here, but true to my word, and anxious to return to my bed, I agree to such an establishment for a trial period of six months. Justin leaves to 'hang a few thoughts on some ears he knows' and I retire again between the blankets not entirely sure whether the whole incident has not been some hideous dream.

Viola Odette has invited Roger and myself to lunch. I am nonplussed to discover that Mr Bridger is also there. No doubt this is an attempt by the Odette sisters to heal the rift that has developed between him and ourselves. Still, if only for the sake of the Cox's apples, I am willing to accept a truce. Normally Sunday lunch at the Odettes' is a roast but, as Letitia proudly announces, today, in honour of our recent visit to France, the menu will be *à la française*. I wonder whether, in trying to cement peace between ourselves and Mr

Bridger, a celebration of French cuisine is entirely appropriate. The first course is *escargots*, which I remember from Fontainebleau, and I remark how surprising it is that something which looks like a plate of snails should taste so nice. For some reason I lose my appetite on being told by Letitia that they *are* snails. Mr Bridger, sharing my astonishment, complains that this illustrates precisely the trouble with foreign food: that you do not know what you are eating. Viola, anxious to save the situation, replies that it is not foreign food, and that she collected the snails from the garden herself that morning. Nobody seemed particularly anxious to try the *coq au vin* until Letitia broke an embarrassing silence by explaining that the chicken used was one supplied by her friend Norman who, the dreaded Newcastle's disease having receded, was once again in the poultry business. Its antecedents adequately explained, I am pleased to say that everybody ate heartily.

Over coffee, mellowed by time and half a bottle of turnip liqueur, Mr Bridger apologizes for his behaviour in France and agrees to settle the outstanding garage bill. I take twelve pounds sixty pence, plus V.A.T., and promise to return his corkscrew at the earliest opportunity. On the way home I am struck by a pang of conscience: even as I was taking Mr Bridger's money I was aware that Roger had, in response to an appeal for useful implements to send to the third world, given this item to the lady from War on Want yesterday morning.

Monday, 16 July

Roger, who ate most of his *escargots* before discovering their true identity, looks very grey this morning and complains of a stomach-ache. I really think we must do something to stop Viola's forays into European gastronomy before somebody is killed.

The post brings a letter from Michael Cooper-Evans, the Managing Director of J. Walter Thompson, the advertising agency. As Sir Stephen Roberts, Chairman of the Milk Marketing Board, advised, I approached them to see if they would be prepared to help build up a market for 'Le Fromage européen'. Unfortunately Mr Cooper-Evans has had to decline our offer as his company already handles the products of Kraft Foods Limited. He is most kind, however, in offering us the use of a slogan which he says occurred to him while reading our letter: 'Le Fromage européen: Not for any Tom, Dick or Henri'. I like this very much, and I cannot blame them for their decision. I dare say it is easier to sell those little triangular cheeses made by Kraft (for which I myself must confess a weakness) than to persuade the populace to buy vast quantities of red globules of fat with a pungent smell of herring.

To buck Roger up I suggest that while I am in town this afternoon I will make inquiries about a licence for our new radio station. When I do so the girl behind the counter in the post office looks at me blankly but, explaining that she is new to the job, searches through all her forms. It becomes apparent that should I desire to license a dog or tax a motorcycle, then she has the appropriate paperwork, but given that my wish is, in Justin's words, 'to get it on with the great wide world' she is sorry but she cannot help me. One of her colleagues suggests that I write to the Independent Broadcasting Authority, which he thinks organizes such things. I shall do this, but I fear that Roger, who on my return I find feeling better and already setting about the construction of his twin turntable, will not be happy with the delay.

Tuesday, 17 July

Despite my having sent two reminders, there is still no word from the European Investment Bank on finance for our Euro-tower. This is most worrying, as I was hoping to get the foundations in before the beginning of the bad weather. Letitia Odette says the delay may be explained by our application having been misfiled or landing on the desk of somebody who

J. WALTER THOMPSON COMPANY
LIMITED
40 Berkeley Square, London W1X 6AD. Tel: 01-629 9496
Telegraphic address: Thomertwal, London Telex: 22871

5th July, 1984

W. Morgan Petty Esq.,
3 Cherry Drive,
Canterbury,
Kent

Dear Mr. Morgan Petty,

I'm afraid we're unable to take up the exciting challenge thrown down in your letter of 29th June.

Advertising agencies are not allowed to work on competing products; unfortunately, your "Fromage Europeen" clashes directly with the fine range of cheeses we present to the public on behalf of Kraft Foods Limited.

However, a slogan did occur to me as I was reading your letter and I mention it for what it is worth:-

"LE FROMAGE EUROPEEN : NOT FOR ANY TOM, DICK OR HENRI"

Good luck. We're rooting for you.

Yours sincerely,

Michael Cooper-Evans

is still on holiday. As usual, her superior knowledge of financial matters is of great assistance to me, and she suggests that I write to Mr Nigel Lawson. Apparently, by virtue of his position as Chancellor of the Exchequer, he has a seat on the board of this bank, and I therefore ask him if, the next time he attends a board meeting, in between explaining to the other members why his economic policies have been such a dismal failure, he could pop down the corridor and have a word with the manager to hurry along a decision over the financing of our project.

Letitia also suggests that, just in case the Investment Bank cannot help, we should look into alternative forms of funding, for example issuing something called our own 'paper' (by which I think she means shares) in the Euro-tower project. Such 'paper' could be underwritten by the expected profits on Ingrid's nut cutlets in the revolving vegetarian restaurant, our surplus vegetables, and their home-made jam and pasties. She says that she has every confidence that such a 'flotation' would be successful. On the other hand, I am not sure. Having no head for high finance I know little about the stock market, but I do remember seeing a long time ago some newsreel footage of American investors, newly impoverished by the Wall Street crash, jumping from the tops of tall buildings. What would happen, I ask, if the bottom were to fall out of the European pastie market, or there was a sharp decline in the demand for vegetarian meals? I hardly relish the prospect of having to do the honourable thing by leaping from the chimneystack on to the patio below. I do not doubt Letitia's abilities but, mindful of the discrepancy between her forecast and our experience over the industrial zone, I think I shall consult an expert. I have therefore written to Mr Paul Neild, at the stockbrokers Phillips and Drew. I have seen Mr Neild on several budget-day programmes, and he certainly seems to know what he is talking about. I have asked him to examine the feasibility of Letitia's proposals and to let me have his considered opinion as to whether such a flotation underwritten by vegetables, pasties and blackcurrant jam would be successful.

Wednesday, 18 July

A letter from the regimental headquarters of the Coldstream Guards. It seems that, much as they would like to come, their diary is full for the next year or so, but they helpfully suggest a choir and drum majorettes to take their place. This indeed may be the answer, both providing a colourful spectacle and, if we can recruit suitable candidates locally, saving a great deal on travel costs.

The house is once again overwhelmed by electronic music as Justin and Roger listen, with the volume turned full up, to Radio One. I wonder why it is that all the 'disc jockeys' on this particular channel sound as though they have graduated from the ranks of the castrati section of a poor-quality music society? Still, as Justin never ceases to tell me, the success or failure of the venture we are about to undertake will depend entirely on his and Roger's being 'hip' and able to 'connect with the kids out there on the streets'. Does he, I wonder, mean that our potential audience will consist of the sort of young man who certainly connected with me by skating into my path on the way to the shop, oblivious of everything except the music coming through the earphones of his radio? If so, I am somewhat perplexed, for, arrogant though it may seem, I cannot see such persons being enormously interested in the injustices brought about by Common Market fishing policy or our failure to secure a lupin subsidy. After all, one of the vital elements in the function of this radio station will be propaganda, or, as I like to call it, following the example of governments throughout the world, 'objective reporting on a balanced scale with regard to the national interest and those of our allies', and naturally I would like such 'objective reporting' to reach people of influence. I voice these concerns to Justin, who says he understands completely, and as for reaching people of influence I can rest assured that he knows for a fact that Simon Le Bon and Bob Geldof listen a great deal to Radio One, and once our station is on the air, if we get the right sort of 'sounds', they will also doubtless listen to us. Who Mr Le Bon and Mr Geldof are I am not entirely sure. Still, they sound foreign, and for all I know may be connected with the Common Market. What is more, given my ignorance on the subject, I must trust, however unwillingly, to Justin's judgement.

Thursday, 19 July

For the third day running the house vibrates to the sound of loud rock music, and it is to my intense relief when Justin, seeking to increase the volume still further by the addition of an extra speaker, overloads the system, plunging the house into darkness. Being unable to boil the kettle and make a cup of tea seems a small price to pay for this blessed silence. I am very surprised by Justin's whole approach to this radio business, having always visualized the voices behind the microphones at the B.B.C. as emanating from individuals in evening dress sipping Lapsang Souchong in between movements of the great symphonies, not rushing about in T-shirts bearing the legend ELVIS IS KING, with watches strung about their necks on leather thongs and apparently trying to outdo each other in verbal inanity. Nor am I very keen on the name they have chosen for the new station: 'Radio Strawberry (because of its proximity to the Cambridge favourites), the Voice of Free Cherry Drive'.

Certainly Roger is very taken with his new role as a 'D.J.' and says that he hopes, under Justin's tutelage, to become the next John Peel 'playing the sounds that everybody wants to hear'. I have to confess that, despite his obvious eminence in the world of popular music, I have not heard of Mr Peel, and I try and persuade Roger to consider following more the example of Richard Baker, whom I remember first from reading the news and now as the presenter of *Baker's Dozen*, a programme I very much enjoy while doing the hoovering.

From: Major D N Thornewill

REGIMENTAL HEADQUARTERS
COLDSTREAM GUARDS
WELLINGTON BARRACKS
BIRDCAGE WALK
LONDON SW1E 6HQ

TELEPHONE
01-930 4466

DO/7101

W Morgan Petty Esq
3 Cherry Drive
CANTERBURY
Kent   9 July 1984

Dear Mr Morgan Petty,

Thank you for your letter of 15 June. I am delighted
that you are taking your new responsibilities so
seriously, as we all know how important your position
in life has become.

I am sorry to have taken so long to reply but it has
proved to be extremely difficult to find out the true
cost of a Guard of Honour (complete with a Band),
especially as you would obviously want the cost to be
quoted in surplus Cos lettuces, together with any
spare homemade jams and pasties which the Odette
sisters may not have sold but which they might like
to present as mementos of the great occasion.
Unfortunately you have neglected to give me a date,
so I am unable to say whether anyone could be spared
on the date you have in mind. Our diaries are pretty
full for the next year or two, so things do not look
too hopeful.

1

I am, however, reliably informed that Canterbury has
a fairly well thought of choir and corps of Drum
Majorettes, and that except for Saturdays and Sundays
(and during school hours), they are readily available
and willing to have a go at almost anything. Being
what they are, I believe that the Drum Majorettes would
much prefer to be associated with lupins rather than
lettuces, which tend to have a Bunny-girl flavour about
them.

I hope that all goes well on THE DAY, and all here join
me in wishing you and your team the best of British
luck.

Yours sincerely,

Thomeville

Mr Baker fits in very much better with my idea of black tie and Lapsong Souchong, and so I have written to him on Roger's behalf to see whether, given his vast experience, he could offer our aspiring D.J. a few tips on broadcasting to the world. The post brings a note from the Office of the Prime Minister of Trinidad and Tobago to the effect that he has delegated the matter of agricultural exports (callaloo and sapodillas) to us here at 3 Cherry Drive, under the provisions of the Lomé Convention, to two of his ministers. I am pleased to hear this, and I am sure it will not be long before we receive our first parcel containing these items.

Saturday, 21 July

I am dismayed to find that the noticeboard in the garden has been commandeered: my own CHERRY DRIVE EURODIRECTIVE NUMBER FIFTEEN dealing with the vexed question of Hyacinths: vegetable or flower? has had pinned over it a note summoning one and all to a scheduling meeting for Radio Strawberry tomorrow morning. With the lack of sleep from the constant sound of loud music, bits of insulating cable turning up in the most unexpected places, and worst of all Roger's neglect of other, equally important tasks (he overlooked spraying the Victoria plum last Tuesday), I am beginning to wish that I had never agreed to the establishment of a radio station. I make up my mind to speak to Justin on this matter, but no sooner do I get him to myself than he 'lays another really neat idea on me'.

In the post, a letter from the European Court of Auditors. It is so long ago that I had almost forgotten I had written. With the possibility of grants from such diverse areas within the Community, and naturally wishing that everything here at 3 Cherry Drive should be seen to be above board, I was delighted to learn that the Common Market had its own auditors, and approached them to see if they would do our books. I explained that it should not be too arduous a task, as Roger has kept a full account of all of our transactions on an

OFFICE OF THE PRIME MINISTER

WHITEHALL, PORT-OF-SPAIN, TRINIDAD, TRINIDAD AND TOBAGO

July 18, 1984

Mr. W. Morgan Petty,
3, Cherry Drive,
Canterbury,
Kent,
ENGLAND.

Dear Mr. Petty,

I am directed to acknowledge your letter of July 2, 1984, and to inform you that your request has been forwarded to the Minister of Industry, Commerce and Consumer Affairs and the Minister of Agriculture, Lands and Food Production.

Yours sincerely,

M. Brathwaite (Mrs)

Secretary to the Prime Minister

exercise pad he bought in Woolworth's. My one fear was whether the Court of Auditors would think it worth while sending somebody all the way from Luxembourg just to certify our records. For that reason I approached the Camera Club, of which Roger is a prominent member. I know that they have had difficulties with their own book-keeping ever since Mr Noble, who used to make them up, moved to Brighton to live with his sister, and I asked if they would care to share the services of these auditors, their participation and the consequent extra remuneration making the journey a viable proposition. Unfortunately neither the Camera Club nor ourselves will be able to benefit from this arrangement as Mr Shannon, the Assistant to the British Member of the Court, tells us that they already have more books than they can cope with. Perhaps they will be better placed to help us next year.

Their letter does provide one very useful piece of information, explaining as it does that we might qualify for assistance under the new ESPRIT scheme. Roger has been on at me for some time to install a computer, which he insists will help his decision-making on planting and vegetable cultivation. I have resisted this step, fearing firstly that such an acquisition would cause him to spend more than the time saved in the garden sitting in front of what I think is termed the visual display unit, playing electronic ping-pong. However, the second and decisive reason for my refusal was the cost. Still, if we can have this equipment paid for with a grant from the European Community I shall certainly reconsider the matter. To that end I write to Sir Michael Edwardes, Chairman of International Computers, to inquire as to the cost of a suitable piece of 'hardware' and the appropriate 'software'. I suppose it is too much to hope that they have any programmes on broad-bean cultivation, but I ask anyway.

Sunday, 22 July

Naturally I had thought that I would be the chairman of the radio-scheduling meeting, and so I am surprised when Roger

125

| DE EUROPÆISKE FÆLLESSKABER REVISIONSRETTEN | | ΕΥΡΩΠΑΪΚΕΣ ΚΟΙΝΟΤΗΤΕΣ ΕΛΕΓΚΤΙΚΟ ΣΥΝΕΔΡΙΟ |

EUROPÄISCHE GEMEINSCHAFTEN RECHNUNGSHOF

COMUNITÀ EUROPEE CORTE DEI CONTI

EUROPEAN COMMUNITIES COURT OF AUDITORS

COMMUNAUTÉS EUROPÉENNES COUR DES COMPTES

EUROPESE GEMEENSCHAPPEN REKENKAMER

Mr W. Morgan Petty,   20 July 1984
3 Cherry Drive,
Canterbury,
KENT

Dear Mr Morgan Petty,

    I am replying to your recent letter to Sir Norman Price who retired
from the Court of Auditors at the end of last year and is presently tending
his garden somewhere on the south coast of England.

    I must say that I found your letter most refreshing, arriving as it did
at our busiest time of year - the gestation period for the Court's annual
report.

    I gather from your letter that your vegetable production is booming
and producing a considerable surplus. No doubt this is partly the result
of the high degree of confidence which producers of agricultural produce
have developed in the context of a European-wide common market. However
I am afraid that in the last year or two surpluses have gone a little out
of fashion and I would even go so far as to venture the opinion that
Mrs Barbara Castle's advice about lupins may have been rather overtaken by
events. In the present financial climate you might be better advised to
stay indoors and play with your home computer in the hope that you might
qualify for assistance under the new "ESPRIT" scheme which has just been
set up by the European Commission to help Europeans to compete with the
Japanese and Americans in the field of information technology research.

    As far as "doing your books" is concerned I am sorry to have to say
that we have already more books to do than we can hope to cope with. Perhaps
if you ask your friend who takes the Financial Times she might be able to
suggest a suitable alternative in the United Kingdom.

    In the meantime may I take this opportunity of wishing you continuing
success in your business ventures.

                                          Yours sincerely,

                                          Alan Shannon
                                          Assistant to the British Member

                                          29, RUE ALDRINGEN
                                          1118 LUXEMBOURG

                                  TÉLÉPHONE 4773-1 / TÉLEX : 3512 EURAUD LU
                                  ADRESSE TÉLÉGRAPHIQUE : EURAUDIT LUXEMBOURG

suggests that this position be filled by a vote. He and Ingrid vote for Justin on the grounds of his greater experience while the Odette sisters, loyal to the last, vote for me. The casting vote is Mr Bridger's. He hesitates for a moment and then, I suspect remembering the business over the corkscrew, votes for Justin. With a great deal of dignity in defeat, I take the seat at the back as Justin explains briefly that he wants the station to be 'right on' and 'cutting it', and asks for programme suggestions.

After three quarters of an hour several very positive ideas have emerged. Justin has agreed to give over a 'prime time slot' to the Women's group, WAVE, where Ingrid can read her poems interspersed with music from their recently formed feminist xylophone band. Mr Bridger has undertaken to go 'on air' once a week and explain the problems of disease in cultivated plants, beginning with *alternaria zinniae* or seedling blight. Viola will talk on cookery and Letitia is anxious to host a programme of 'new wave' music. Everybody, including Justin, seems somewhat startled by her choice. Does she, he asks, know anything about new wave music? As it turns out she is quite an authority on the subject, a result of the newspaper boy regularly putting *Melody Maker* through her letter-box instead of *My Weekly*. I decline the offer of a programme, explaining that with all my other commitments I just would not have the time. I do however agree to help Roger with the production of 'In the Garden Discs', a programme he intends modelling on 'Desert Island Discs', where Mr Roy Plomley interviews well-known people about their reactions to being stranded on a desert island and which eight gramophone records they would choose to take with them as company into this exile. The title is quite appropriate, as Roger plans to interview his guests on how they would cope with being locked up indefinitely in our old garden shed, down by the leylandii, and which recordings they would choose to help cope with the onset of claustrophobia. Instead of using the sound of seagulls to open the programmes as

Mr Plomley does, Roger has borrowed Ingrid's cassette player and recorded a first-rate selection of blackbirds and thrushes.

After supper, when we have the house to ourselves, we draw up a list of people that Roger wishes to invite on to the first of his programmes. We both agree that he should seek to open with something spectacular and, for that reason, extend invitations to His Holiness Pope John Paul II, the Archbishop of Canterbury and Lord Olivier. Aware that these are very important people and likely to have diaries that will be full for some time, I suggest to Roger that he makes contingency plans and invites someone less well known but who could fill in in an emergency should his more eminent guests not be able to make it. We therefore also extend invitations to Mr Dickie Fountain, an old army friend of Mr Bridger's from the Catering Corps who, after his demobilization, set out across the Middle East on a motorbike and has a wealth of anecdotes, including one very funny story about a hotel in Alexandria and a waiter with a glass eye and a wooden leg which has the Odette sisters in stitches every time he tells it, and to Olive Matterhorn, a friend of his late mother, who spent most of her childhood in West Africa and has some really fascinating recollections about the many diseases you can catch in that part of the world.

Monday, 23 July

In all the programme planning that has taken place, one very important factor has been overlooked. We do not have any records. Roger says that he is sure there are some in the attic, but after a thorough search he returns with precisely two. The first is Max Bygraves singing 'You're a Pink Toothbrush I'm a Blue Toothbrush' and the second is The Springfields holding forth with a Christmas song entitled 'Bambino'. Roger's often repeated aim is to 'spin the sounds that everybody wants to hear', but, having listened to these records, I fear he will be spinning sounds that most people would run a mile to avoid. Surprisingly, Justin seems unconcerned by the news, and says that we will just have to follow the example of Radio Leviathan and play our two records alternately, varying the speed and volume. Apparently, faced with a similar problem, his former station spent a whole week re-playing just one single, by somebody called Rod Stewart, in this way and nobody complained. Tapping his nose gently in the fashion of one privy to life's little secrets, Justin explains that as long as you remember to tell people the sounds are different, they don't notice, as it is a well known fact amongst practitioners of his art that nobody really listens anyway.

Using Roger's ageing Dansette record player (the twin deck he has been working on needs some modification as, for some reason, the turntables spin in different directions), we test this theory. I must admit that, at half speed and with the volume full up, I find it difficult to distinguish between The Springfields' message of Christmas cheer and some of the stuff I have been recently subjected to on Radio One. Furthermore, at twice the speed I find Mr Bygraves is greatly improved. While this might provide a short-term solution to our problem, what, I ask Justin, is Roger to do for 'In the Garden Discs', where he will need at least eight records? What would happen if the Pope should ask for a Gregorian chant or Ave Maria? We could hardly expect His Holiness to be fooled by turning the volume right down and putting Mr Bygraves on thirty-three revolutions per minute.

Justin sees my point and suggests we resolve the difficulty by getting on somebody's 'freebie list'. Apparently it is quite common for radio stations to receive free records for promotional purposes, the idea being that playing them encourages listeners to buy. I therefore write to Mr Richard Branson at Virgin Records. According to Justin, Mr Branson seems to own practically everything in the pop world, and so I ask if he could spare a few records to help get Radio Strawberry off the ground. I am not quite sure what sort of records Mr Branson's company produces. It would be too much to hope, I suppose, that Max Jaffa, a favourite of mine, is among their artistes. However, mindful of Roger's choice of guests, I expect that we will be on safe ground with the classics, Beethoven, Brahms, etc., where Lord Olivier is concerned, and I imagine that the Pope will be more than happy with recordings of choirs of nuns singing their heads off. On the question of the Archbishop of Canterbury, Roger said he knew nothing of Dr Runcie's taste in music, but he thought the Primate of England looked like he might be a Barry Manilow fan, and so we shall consider getting some of these and maybe a little 'heavy metal'.

Wednesday, 25 July

A letter from Mr Robert Muldoon, the Prime Minister of New Zealand. It is very brief and contains no information at all about the availability of fleeces. I am still puzzling over this when Roger arrives. At the sight of him all thoughts of Mr Muldoon's missive are driven from my mind. He is wearing an earring. At first I pretend not to notice, but so prominent is this object, shaped like a star and with what appears to be a rhinestone in the middle, that in the end I am forced to mention it. He tells me that it is a necessary part of his new image. Fortunately he has a great deal to do in the garden this afternoon, and so I am spared the embarrassment of its continued presence. Viola Odette, whose legs are much improved since she bought herself a sun lamp, drops in for some advice from Roger on her clematis, which it seems is not doing very well this year. Remembering his earring, and wishing to save us all from an embarrassing situation, I lie and tell her that he is at the library and, changing the subject, show her my note from New Zealand. Viola does not share my surprise at its brevity, explaining that less than a fortnight ago a general election was held in that country and Mr Muldoon is no longer the Prime Minister. I think he could have mentioned that in his letter, but as Viola points out he may still be feeling too low to put the fact down in black and white. No doubt he will have passed the details of our request on to his successor, but just to be on the safe side and to ensure the arrival of our fleeces at the earliest opportunity I shall drop Mr Lange a line myself.

Viola is about to go when Roger appears at the kitchen door with a handful of early carrots. He looks somewhat confused when I express surprise that he has returned from the library without my noticing, but before he can reply Viola interrupts to compliment him on his earring. What I had thought made him look like a rather down-on-his-luck pirate does, according to Viola, a great deal to set off the masculinity of his looks. What is more, she tells him that she too has an odd earring, white gold in the shape of a dolphin, but having lost the other one it is of no use to her, and should he like it to wear, alternately with his rhinestone-embedded star, he is most welcome. Roger thanks her very much and, parched from his work in the garden, asks if anyone would like some tea. I decline, seeking some time alone in the lounge where, confused, I partake of something very much stronger.

Thursday, 26 July

A letter from the Chairman of the Post Office outlining the difficulties that we face in producing our own commemorative stamps. Sir Ronald's office informs me that should we wish to regard ourselves as an independent sovereign state for the purposes of issuing such stamps, then we would have to convince the one hundred and sixty-six countries in the Universal Postal Union of the strength of our case. However, I also note that the next meeting of this organization, where we could put forward our plans, is in San Diego, in 1989. It may well be that this delay is a blessing in disguise, as, overwhelmed with all his other activities, Roger has not yet found the time to redesign our stamps, the first proofs of which were so thoughtlessly destroyed by Mr Oliver. Nor, as he points out, have we yet received permission from Ms Germaine Greer to use her profile. Despite these difficulties I resolve, in preparation for the meeting in California, where I am sure that we will be welcomed with open arms into the ranks of

Prime Minister
Wellington
New Zealand

23 July 1984

Mr W.M. Petty,
3 Cherry Drive,
Canterbury,
Kent,
ENGLAND

Dear Mr Petty,

I acknowledge receipt of your letter of
7 July 1984.

Yours sincerely,

R.D. Muldoon

L'Union Postale Universelle, to drop a line to each of the members of this organization making them aware of the position. However I am in something of a quandary as to whose stamps we should stick on to the envelopes, ours or theirs.

Thursday, 2 August

I am driven from the house, not this time by the raucous sounds of Radio Caroline but by the rehearsal of the feminist xylophone band whom Justin is putting through their paces. When I looked in, Roger, still displaying his earring, was nodding in time as the three young women tapped out with remarkable resonance the 1812 overture. My doubts that this was not entirely what the public wanted were brushed aside by Justin, who tells me that xylophones are 'very big' on the west coast. I have a cousin who lives in Weston-super-Mare, and I cannot recall him ever mentioning it.

It being such a nice day I take refuge in the garden. I am surprised that the Independent Broadcasting Authority have not replied to my letter requesting an application form for a radio station licence. Perhaps the man in the Post Office was right, and we do not need one after all. Still, it is better to be safe than sorry, and so I drop a line to Mr David Mellor M.P., at the Home Office, to ask him to clarify the position, as it would be most unfortunate if Roger was playing Mr Bygraves on whatever speed when a detector van turned up. Letitia arrives breathless at the front door. Apparently she was listening to a new programme on the Home Service, called *Carousel* or *Merrygoround* or something of that kind, introduced by Richard Baker (what an enormously busy man he is), and according to Letitia Mr Baker asked that I telephone him in the studio. Unfortunately by the time she arrived the programme was over. Not that we would have had much success earlier, not being on the telephone at home and the call box in the Whitstable Road having been jammed up with an Irish florin for some days. I do not tell Roger of his brief

The Post Office

Royal Mail
National Girobank

Christina Lomas
Personal Assistant to
The Chairman

Post Office Headquarters
St Martins le Grand
LONDON
EC1A 1PG

Telephone 01-432 3441

Mr W Morgan Petty
3 Cherry Drive
CANTERBURY
Kent
CT2 8HF

25 July 1984

Dear Mr. Petty,

You wrote to the Chairman of the Post Office, Sir Ronald Dearing on 12 June about a project which could have far reaching consequences for the Common Market and the international postal community.

As you will appreciate, Sir Ronald, in addition to replying to letters from our customers, who are of course, always right, has to spend some time actually running the Postal Business and I, Christina Lomas, his Personal Assistant, am replying on his behalf.

Your letter touches on some aspects, which have nothing to do with the Post Office and which we, therefore, are not strictly competent to deal with. In fact, some of our critics have gone as far as to question our competence to deal with postal matters.

None the less, I wish you every success in keeping your address nuclear free, in respect of nuclear missiles which may be delivered to 3 Cherry Drive, CANTERBURY, Kent, CT2 8HF. As I am writing from Central London, this arrangement would be convenient for me as well. If you are unfortunately, not successful, there could be a case for an issue of stamps which would be commemorative in a rather special way.

I was interested in your scheme to sell a range of vegetables and groceries to the Common Market. You might find it helpful to enquire about the size of the jam lake and pasties mountain before going too far. Although some countries outside the Common Market are prepared to buy butter from Europe at knock-down prices, I am not sure about the demand for jam and pasties. Could the Odette Sisters turn their hand to Vodka? In which case check first with Customs and Excise.

You ask whether it would be possible for the Post Office to issue a licence to you to issue postal stamps to commemorate pasties, if you paid the Post Office to sort and deliver letters with such stamps. There are a few impediments. If you regard yourself as an independent sovereign state, with the right to issue stamps, you would have to convince the 166 countries who belong to the Universal Postal Union, of the viability of your address as an independent postal administration and your ability to pay the annual subscription which is a minimum of 17,500 Swiss Francs.

There may well be a Common Market grant to cover this expenditure; application forms should be available at your local Post Office. Unfortunately, the quinquennial congress of the UPU has just finished in Hamburg, and there will not be another opportunity for you to present your application until 1989 in San Diego.

Additionally, the depth and inpenetrability of some foreign postal bureacracies is such as to put that of the British Post Office on a par with your local fish and chip shop. That problem solved, the principal remaining difficulty would be to placate competitor countries who produce stamps for philatelists. The British Post Office is moderate in its methods in dealing with this competition, rarely going further than to obliterate completely the more attractive stamps used on foreign mail when they reach our sorting offices, but others may not be as reasonable in their attitude.

Alternatively, if you sell your postal service for at least a pound per letter, you do not need a licence and we should not take offence. We would be happy to squeeze you out of this market with our much better service.

Regretfully, unless you were a foreign Postal Administration, we could not accept stamps with the profile of the person you suggest, because the one we use currently is much better known all over the world.

You could use "pseudo" stamps in addition to proper Post Office first and second class stamps, if they comply with our requirements about size, shape, colour and position of these on the envelope. These regulations are of such stupefying complexity that I shall not go into detail now.

I think your best approach is to confine your postal service to letters posted in 3 Cherry Drive for delivery to the same address. I know that this will restrict the scope of the service you can give, but will have the advantage of being cheap, quick and hopefully reliable.

I hope that Roger will again come to help you with the garden and that Ingrid will always be ready with sympathetic advice.

Meanwhile, pending the decision about your future postal status, I have used the address we recommend. You will note that we have included your postcode. It is important to be scrupulous about such basic details, if you hope to compete with such an efficient service as the British Post Office.

Yours sincerely,

Christina Lomas

ICL Public Limited Company
Bridge House Putney Bridge Fulham London SW6 3JX
Telephone 01-788 7272 Telex 22971

From the Chairman's Office

W Morgan Petty Esq
3 Cherry Drive
Canterbury
Kent

30 July 1984

Dear Mr Petty

Sir Michael has asked me to thank you so much for your
letter of 27 July.

Your enquiry has been passed to the appropriate executive in
ICL who will reply direct.

Yours sincerely

C A WATKIN (Miss)
Secretary to Sir Michael Edwardes

Registered office ICL House Putney London SW15 1SW   Registered in England No 142200

New Zealand High Commission

Office of the Minister (Commercial)
and Senior Trade Commissioner
New Zealand House
Haymarket
London SW1Y 4TQ
Tel: 01-930 8422 Telex: 24368

27 July 1984   Reference: TC 95/2

Mr W.Morgan Petty
3 Cherry Drive
Canterbury
Kent

Dear Mr Petty

The High Commissioner has asked me to thank you for your
letter of 7 July and to reply to it.

We appreciate your letting us know that you have personally
taken over from the Foreign and Commonwealth Office the
responsibility of dealing with the European Common Market,
and we wish you well in disposing of your home-grown
vegetable surplus. The disposal by the Common Market of its
subsidised agricultural surpluses, especially dairy, poses
major problems for New Zealand in third country markets, and
every initiative to sell this produce within member states is
to be encouraged. From what you say, your own production
will be sold locally, and it is certainly useful to have in
close proximity such supplementary outlets as the Odette
sisters.

Naturally we would be delighted if your market were to include
such readily available New Zealand agricultural items as
butter and cheese, lamb, apples and kiwifruit, and we can put
you in touch with supply sources once your plans advance a
little further. On the inedible side, you mention specifically
sheep fleeces to help sustain the renewed spinning activity of
the Misses Odette, and the attachment to this letter suggests
some UK and New Zealand contacts for these products.
Incidentally, New Zealand is neither classified as a developing
country nor covered by the provisions of the Lome Convention.

In response to your request for delivery dates, I should point
out that the High Commission does not hold commercial stocks
of our excellent agricultural products. Quite apart from
diplomatic prohibitions, our accommodation here in the Haymarket
would not, to say the least, be up to the task.

We hope that this information will be initially helpful, and
extend you, and Roger your horticulturalist, best wishes for
every success in your new business venture.

Yours sincerely

D.J.Walker
Minister (Commercial)

fame as I am sure he will be most disappointed at having missed the mention of his name, especially in a week when, his attention diverted elsewhere, the aphis have made rather a mess of his imperial green longpods. I have however written another letter to the B.B.C. in the hope that Mr Baker might mention him again next Thursday, when I will make sure he is near a wireless tuned in to this new programme. I have also sent him with Letitia and Viola's best regards a jar of newly made raspberry jam.

Monday, 6 August

There are three letters in the post today. The first is a response from the New Zealand High Commission which provides some most useful information about the products of that country. I am however surprised to learn that New Zealand is not classified as a developing country or covered by the provisions of the Lomé Convention. From some of the photographs Roger's brother Malcolm, who emigrated to that country and is a hairdresser in Wellington, has sent home, I can't say it looked very developed to me. Still, we shall not hold that against them if the quality of their sheep's fleeces and the appropriately named kiwifruit is as good as we have been led to believe. The second missive is from Mr Branson at Virgin Records, who has passed our request on to his Promotions department. No doubt we shall soon, with their help, be enjoying the exotic sounds of the rumba from Max Jaffa and his orchestra. The final letter is from the United States Secretary of Defence, Mr Caspar Weinberger. Unfortunately his schedule is such that he will not be able to take up our offer of observer status at the Lupin Talks. This will come as a disappointment to Roger, who also intended using this opportunity to invite Mr Weinberger on to 'In the Garden Discs'. I too share this disappointment, having undertaken a small wager with Letitia Odette on Mr Weinberger's musical preferences. She expressed the view that he was probably an

Ella Fitzgerald man, but I remained convinced that his taste was more for *Götterdämmerung*.

On the question of the talks, Roger appears to have solved the entertainment problem. He tells me that a Mr Robert Maxwell, who has recently taken over the *Daily Mirror* newspaper, is quite an exponent of housey-housey, and seems intent on turning it into the national pastime. What better way for us to amuse our guests than to organize a game of this? I shall therefore write to Mr Maxwell seeking his help. I have also asked if he is in a position to lend us one of those little contraptions that blows air up through a tube, scattering the numbered balls at random. It would also be of tremendous help if he had a dozen or so little boards with counters. Naturally, as the equipment will be his, I have extended an invitation for him to join us, if he is not too busy, and it may even be that he would enjoy calling out the numbers himself.

Friday, 17 August

I have received from Mr Seamus Burke, at the Electoral Reform Society, confirmation of the validity of my method of election to the European Parliament. Now that any shadow of doubt on this question has been removed I shall make arrangements to journey to Strasbourg at the earliest opportunity and take the seat in this institution that is rightfully mine. The second post brings a letter from Mr David Lange, the Prime Minister of New Zealand, who says that he is pleased to see that the British people can retain their sense of humour in the face of the absurdities of the Common Market. Absurdities, whatever can he mean?

Virgin Group Limited

95-99 Ladbroke Grove, London W11 1PG
Tel: 01-229 1282 Telex: 8954617
Reg No. in England. 1560894

30th July 1984

Ms. W. Morgan Petty,
3, Cherry Drive,
Canterbury,
KENT

Dear Ms. Petty,

Thanks for your pleasant letter.

I wish you good luck and every success with your various
ventures, and in the meantime, have passed your letter
on to our Promotions department to see if there is any
way in which they may be able to help you.

Thanks again for taking the time to write.

Regards,

Richard Branson,
CHAIRMAN

July 30, 1984

Mr. W. Morgan Petty
3, Cherry Drive
Canterbury, Kent.
United Kingdom

Dear Mr. Petty:

Secretary Weinberger has asked me to thank you for your thoughtful letter of June 28, and for your kind invitation to join you at 3, Cherry Drive for the upcoming meeting of Heads of State from those countries who are members of the Common Market.

He was flattered that you thought to include him among Heads of State, and he is greatly interested in European affairs. I must point out, however, that in his position as the Secretary of Defense, he rarely has the occasion to get into matters such as vegetable trade, or pasties and jams. In addition, his schedule is such that it isn't going to be possible for him to be in Europe at any time in the near future. Therefore, he will be unable to attend, but please be assured of his appreciation of your thoughtfulness in inviting him.

Sincerely,

Kay D. Leisz

Kay D. Leisz
Confidential Assistant to the
Secretary of Defense

Telex: 8812703 (LONSEC)
Tel: 01-928 9407-8

THE
ELECTORAL REFORM
SOCIETY

6 Chancel Street, Blackfriars, London SE1 0UX.

President: The Hon. Dr. Garret FitzGerald, T.D.

From the Chief Executive: Seamus Burke (Direct Line: 01-928 1622)

W. Morgan Petty, Esq.,   10 August 1984
3, Cherry Drive,
Canterbury, Kent.

Dear Mr. Morgan Petty,

My absence has delayed a reply to your letter of 12 July.
I am fascinated, of course, by your decision to join the
Common Market and to be represented in the European
Parliament.

Your wisdom in using the single transferable vote for
your election was commendable but ties can be a problem
when the candidates constitute the electorate. You are
being hard on Roger for behaving as a politician!

Now, to that toss of a coin to break the tie. Yes, it
is perfectly proper but that is only one way. Your
rules could have permitted seniority to be the determinant!
Frankly, I don't think poor Roger stands a chance against
such a sagacious politician as W. Morgan Petty.

Bon voyage!

Yours sincerely,

SEAMUS BURKE

The Electoral Reform Society of Great Britain and Ireland Limited
Limited by Guarantee and registered in London No. 958404. Registered Office: 6 Chancel Street, Blackfriars, London SE1 0UX.

15 August 1984

Mr W Morgan Petty
3, Cherry Drive
Canterbury
Kent
GREAT BRITAIN

Dear Mr Petty

Thank you for your letter of 27 July 1984.

I am pleased to see that the British people can retain
their sense of humour in the face of the absurdities of
the Common Market.

Yours sincerely

David Lange

Lambeth Palace, SE1 7JU.

16th August 1984

Dear W. Morgan Petty,

    I am writing to acknowledge your letter of the
21st July to the Archbishop of Canterbury. I am sorry
you have not received a reply before this. Unfortunately,
your letter arrived when the Archbishop was in Nigeria.
He is now away from Lambeth Palace for a short summer
break.

    However, I am sure the Archbishop will thoroughly
enjoy reading your letter on his return and that he will
appreciate its finer points.

    I have been delighted to hear you warmly referred
to on Radio 4 as I drive to Lambeth Palace in the
mornings. It cheers up the journey to hear subtle
allusions to your industrious correspondence.

        Yours sincerely,

        Eve Keatley
        Lay Assistant (Communications) to
        The Archbishop of Canterbury

W. Morgan Petty, Esq.,
3, Cherry Drive,
Canterbury,
Kent.

LS

 Ministry of Agriculture, Fisheries and Food
Whitehall Place London SW1A 2HH

Telex 889351   Direct line 01-233   or
                                      Switchboard 01-233 3000

W Morgan Petty Esq   Your reference
3 Cherry Drive
CANTERBURY   Our reference
Kent
                                      Date 21 August 1984

Dear Mr Morgan Petty

I am sorry for the delay in replying to your letters of 26 May and
4 July.

The scheme to which you refer relates to the purchase of milk quotas
from dairy farmers who wish to cease milk production. As neither
you or Roger have kept any dairy cows or produced milk for sale it
would seem most unlikely that you will have a quota to sell and you
will not be able to benefit under this Scheme. One possible consol-
ation however is that the milk now subject to quota arrangements is
the produce of cows. Goats milk does not come within the scope of
these arrangements at present. There is therefore no reason why
Roger need be deprived of the companionship of his much wanted goat
any longer.

                              Yours sincerely

                              J A Sutton
                              Milk 3A

Dear W. Morgan Pelty,   3rd September, 84.

            In regard to your request
for a picture of university self for your stamp,
I find the only thing I can offer is this.
I am the one bending down (to pick up
windfallen apricots.)
            The composition, which is what
you would expect, seeing a professional film-maker
took the snap, could be the basis for a very
intriguing composition, of indubitable
significance.
                                yours,
                                        Germaine Greer

SECRETARIAT OF STATE

VATICAN CITY
7 September 1984

Dear Mr Petty,

   I am writing to acknowledge the letter which you addressed to His Holiness Pope John Paul II. The sentiments which prompted you to write are appreciated, but I regret that it is not possible to comply with your request.

   I have pleasure in informing you that His Holiness invokes upon you God's abundant blessings.

                    Yours sincerely,

                    Monsignor G.B. Re
                    Assessor

Mr W. Morgan Petty
3 Cherry Drive
Canterbury
Kent

Ford Motor Company Limited

Sam Toy
Chairman and Managing Director

Brentwood Essex CM13 3BW
England

2 October 1984

Mr W Morgan Petty
3 Cherry Drive
Canterbury
Kent

Dear Mr Petty:

Thank you for your entrepreneurial letter of 15 July
It brightened a dull day, because the motor industry
faces more risks than opportunities these days and I
have taken the necessary time to give it mature
consideration.

Your question is whether Ford would wish to set up a
manufacturing plant at 3 Cherry Drive, Canterbury on
a site measuring forty feet by ten feet. In theory,
of course, almost any shaped site can be adapted to
car production, but there are certain basic
utilities and facilities that we would insist on
before your garden could be considered.

These are:

    1. Power supply. An extension cord from your
       cloakroom will not be sufficient - you will
       have to put arrangements in hand with your
       local electricity board to supply three-
       phase electricity in substantial quantities.

    2. Water. Several million gallons per day will
       be required - with appropriate drainage
       facilities if your lettuces are not to be
       overwhelmed.

                                Cont.

Registered in England: No. 235446 Registered Office: Eagle Way BRENTWOOD Essex CM13 3BW

3. Transport.

   a) Rail. During the start-up period we would require sufficient flat-car facilities at Canterbury to take some 2000 cars per day. Your neighbours are obviously accommodating, so a siding passing through the gardens of Numbers One, Five etc., would presumably present no problems.

   b) Deep Water. This is vital to our access to the Common Market, which you seem to know a bit about. Probably best addressed by constructing a canal to Whitstable, which you might ask the Government to declare a 'Free Port'. This would have other trading advantages for you, as I am sure Letitia Odette will confirm.

One final thought. Your friend Roger is not entirely correct in his stipulation that, with the aid of micro-chip technology, the entire manufacturing process "can be carried out by a computerised robot no bigger than a hatbox", on which he could do the routine maintenance. Our friends in the unions have quite fixed ideas about manning levels, and Roger would in any case have to join their ranks before he would be allowed to carry out such work.

It is probably best if you resolve these infra-structure and other details before we proceed to further consideration of the matter.

Yours sincerely,

P.S. We are a cost-conscious company. How much are the lettuces?

Mirror Group Newspapers

Holborn Circus London EC1P 1DQ

Switchboard: 01-353 0246
Direct Line: 01-822

Telegrams: Mirror London EC1
Telex: 27286
Fax: 01-353 3429

From the Publisher Robert Maxwell MC

XBL/IRM/MT/SF   16 October 1984

W. Morgan Petty Esq
3 Cherry Drive
Canterbury
KENT

Dear Mr Petty

Thank you for your letter. I instructed my staff to lose no time in
dealing with it.

Despite that, I am informed that we have exactly the contraption you
require for playing housey-housey, and it could be made available
for your collection. Unfortunately, we do not use boards and
counters in our games, but you will find books of cards available
from most good stationers. More important, however, I enclose a
most valuable card, which you should treasure, for our win a million
pounds game "WHO DARES WINS".

You get the heads of state: I'll come along and give away a million
pounds. I guarantee it!!

With best wishes

Robert Maxwell
Publisher

Encl

Mirror Group Newspapers Limited Registered Office: Holborn Circus London EC1P 1DQ. A Company Registered in England (No.168660)

Daily Mirror · Sunday Mirror · Sunday People · Daily Record · Sunday Mail · The Sporting Life